Just Be You

Grow, Embrace, and Celebrate

By Wayne Kaboni

Dedication

I dedicate this book to my children and grandchildren, the gift that I never expected, they are the reason that my heart is full and my spirit smiles. I celebrate every day because of my 5 special gifts my 3 kids (Jazmine, Clinton, & Connor) and my granddaughters River and Aspen. They are the reason that I have positive thoughts and they motivate me to have a full and complete life by watching them grow and develop into amazing human beings.

Thank you, my sweets.

Foreword to Just Be You

Victoria Hale, PhD Laguna Niguel, California, USA July 2023

Wayne and I have been friends for years. We resonated immediately as fellow journeyers. One afternoon, sitting in my living room, I recall speaking with Wayne about various complex issues I was involved with in global health. I spoke for a few minutes, then paused to hear Wayne's thoughts. He smiled gently and got to the gist of my message in a single sentence. He blew me away with his pure and simple distillation of my challenges.

A few months ago, Wayne sent me one of his morning missives via text. It resonated and I asked how this knowing came to him. He writes one of these jewels every morning. I asked him to share with me every day.

JUST – keep it simple, allow the quiet heart to speak.

BE – instead of doing, simply BE in the now.

YOU – wisdom is found within you, not outside of you.

Living as human beings on planet earth has not been joyous for most of us. We all need to heal. Wayne reveals that our most important healing is done within, and that we have the power to heal.

Serious wisdom, tenderized, and flavored with humor; this entry really resonated with me:

"An empty stomach, an empty wallet, and a broken spirit or broken heart can teach you the best lessons in life especially if you have the support of people who love you, your friends, your coworkers and sometimes even your family lol."

I can see a mischievous smile on Wayne's face with his last word!

Authenticity is rare. Wayne is vulnerable and intimate. He demonstrates respect for the soul. As long, as we are still capable of breathing, we have free will:

"Sometimes we are so tired that we don't know who or where we are, this past year, I realize Two types of tired one that requires rest and one that requires peace. I chose peace."

Wisdom keepers choose the path of peace.

We all need to pause and contemplate our existence, how we show up in life. Stepping out of our comfort zones and taking risks can free us. It takes courage to bear witness to our shadow selves.

Everything we seek is already within us. There are no more gurus. No more teachers outside of ourselves.

Life often is a boomerang; whatever you put out will come back to you. So have empathy for each other, as we are accompanying each other on this mysterious human soul journey.

Find your soul tribe and keep them close. Share your wisdom in a simple manner, the details can wait. Lift each other up. Together we are better.

The privilege of a lifetime is to become who you truly are – Carl Jung

Introduction

Life is challenging. Along the way, we get bumps and bruises, scrapes and cuts. Most people missed positive reassurance in their lives. The messages in this book have been a great comfort for me to start my day positively.

Many cultures have different cultural notions about grace, positivity, gratitude, and humbleness. My messages are more real for me, and as I started to share them with different people, they became a vital resource for people who are faced with many daily challenges. They didn't resonate with all the people all the time, but often, I would get a message from somebody saying thank you for this. I needed to hear this today.

The messages in this book are more about tools than advice, changing your mindset, and getting clarity for yourself on who, how, and what you want to be. I was part of a seminar where they talked about what you want your headstone to say or what you would like someone to say in your eulogy. I don't like that notion because it doesn't support the idea that life is an ongoing and continued path to growth and instead focuses on the end goal rather than the journey. Over the years, I forgot who I was. I became a hostage to my job as a Senior Manager, and I became a hostage to the notion of protecting my staff and the organization, and I quickly realized that it was a detriment to my personal and psychological health. So, I started to write personal messages to myself to help me reset and set a new path for my spirit, my soul, my heart, and my kids. I've dedicated this book to my kids because they have given me strength.

I am not going to promise you one size fits all solutions when I know that the road you are leading is full of hills and walls. I will not pretend to fill your head with beautiful stories when I know the truth is a bitter one. Instead, I am going to give you tools to change your view and your mindset. Guide you to the answers or options that you seek. This book is my humble attempt to help you make peace with your current situation, find options, and make a choice. The solution or choices do not lie in blind truths or sweet messages drenched in honey. When life gets hard, you need to acknowledge it. Nevertheless, along with that acknowledgment, you need moral support. That is exactly what you are going to find here!

Testimonials

I'd like to say ... These morning affirmations have made me reflect on my life and every morning I look forward to his message. Life changing
Mary

Wayne tumbles private thoughts and feelings into daily reflections. They are fresh and sincere and real. His perspectives are provocative because they're so relatable.
He bravely shares his inside talk with surprising openness that tells you he's comfortable in his own skin and his personal commitment to self-study. His inside voice gently polishes into nuggets of insight that inspire similar reflection and always are underpinned with the reminder just to be you.
Sheryl

I appreciate Wayne's messages. They are daily reminders on how outlook & perspective are key in moving forward. We all face barriers, challenges, and obstacles in life, whether it's work related, family dynamics, & personal friendships, or community politics. His daily messages challenge me in a positive way to rethink my current situation and how to better navigate life with a positive outlook despite what life challenges us with and how it all starts and ends with me.
Pete

"Every morning, I see a genuine and heartfelt message for the day from Wayne. More often than not, the message speaks directly to me and something I'm currently dealing with. It sparks thought or a conversation due to the insight of self-reflection Wayne provides."
Mark

Just Be You provides an opportunity to have one's heart, mind and soul be open to view life with a new perspective. Wayne is raw and honest about the challenges that one's life journey has which allows the reader to be open to viewing their own journey through the lens of thoughtfulness and encouragement. His ability to intertwine his personal, community, and professional experience is magical and shines a light on how to be open to finding joy and discovery in our own path.
Jill

The messages shared by Wayne are almost like a daily meditation, a reminder to be gently open to one's journey and the lessons that come along with it. To pursue your passion and be true to yourself. Always inspirational, uplifting and a wonderful start to the day! Appreciate the gesture, friendship, and depth of insight always!
Gina

Recommendation: "Wherever I am in the world, whether at-home in Squamish, travelling for business or pleasure, I look forward to reading Wayne insightful, grounded thoughts each day. He is a source of retrospect, thoughtfulness and, occasionally, humour that makes a positive impact each day. Thank you, Wayne."
Tom

Just Be You
The Beginning

Good morning! What a good day to be a human being. Embrace the moments that made you an amazing role model, friend, sibling, or parent. Just be yourself and cherish what makes you an amazing human being. Spread your light and energy. Have a great day.

Rise and shine! I hope the sun is shining, your spirit is bright, and your heart is full of hope and joy. Just be you, the bright spirit that everyone enjoys smiling and laughing with, the uplifting energy that makes people want to be around you. Have a great day.

Good morning! Today's just another day to celebrate life. You don't even know this, but by being yourself, you bring a smile to those who need it. With your smile, you give people a reminder they are not alone. You're a positive energy, and your ever-supporting spirit makes the world a better place. Have fun, have a great day and just be you.

Today, the lesson is that hope, and fear are one and the same. Hope gives us a reason to look forward, and fear drives us to move forward. The people with whom I share my life and stories with inspire my hope. Those who bully me challenge me to push through the fear of a better tomorrow. Thanks for being one of the people who drive and inspire me to always hope for the best and drive past the fear. Just be you and have a great day.

You are awake to face the new day. Life is full of challenges and surprises. Enjoy every moment, cherish each second. Because you never get those minutes back, you must embrace them, enjoy them, and cherish them. Give someone a random hug, call an old friend, and catch up. Never waste moments thinking about what you should have done. Just dive in and do it. There are a lot of people who care about you and would move mountains to help you climb the steep, jagged slopes. Ask for help. Don't be shy. There are many ways to turn lemons into several different flavors of good lemonade. Have a great day, and just be you.

Wake up! Wake up because a beautiful life awaits you. Remember that life is full of choices and opportunities, of days of sunshine, full of joy and happiness. So, embrace and cherish those moments of happiness. The body has muscle memory for those moments you need to remember and reach back and learn from the grey. Remember, there's always someone who will take your call, make you laugh and smile, let you cry and scream, or guide you through a new road of choice or happiness with no judgment. Don't be shy. Just ask for an ear or a shoulder. Have a great day, and just be you. You're awesome!

Good morning! If you focus on the hurt, you will continue to suffer. If you focus on the lessons, you will continue to grow. Understand that life is not about being rich, being popular, being the most educated, or being perfect. Life is about being real and authentic. It is about being humble and kind. Just like Tim McGraw's song says, you are awesome. You are a beautiful spirit with a warm heart that always gives and rarely gets, so just be you and have a great day.

Morning sunshine! Don't wait for things to get easier, simpler, or better. Life will always be challenging and complicated. Never stop trusting yourself. Always have faith in you. There are people who believe in you. Your smile brightens up their day. You are an inspiration for many people you don't even know. So, never doubt yourself. Always keep smiling. Have a good day! Just be you.

'It is another day! Today is a reminder that life does have its obstacles and challenges, but are they really that, or are they opportunities in disguise? We are here today as successful individuals with scars, bruises, and broken wings on our journey to a new day. Is the glass half-full or half-empty? Is it just a barrier, an obstacle for which you need a ladder to climb and get past it? Life has taught me to develop a plan that provides one with a strategy, making one realize how to operate that plan. Then, come up with steps based on that strategy to execute the plan.

When you develop these steps, they will help you answer several questions. Such questions include: Why do you need a strategy? What help will you get through it? Who could help you build a better strategy? Remember that establishing these steps and following them will be a challenge but consider it like reading a book, you will not be able to finish reading a book if you do not flip the page and move to the next. Similarly, if you do not conquer the first challenge, the first step based on your developed strategy, you will not be able to conquer the rest of the challenges. I want you to have faith in yourself. I want you to believe in you as I do so that you are strong enough to face these challenges and overcome them because I know that you are awesome. So, just be you!

It is a beautiful morning, remember that there are so many people who love you and want the best for you. So don't focus on those who don't. The underlying message is that an empty stomach, an empty wallet, and a broken spirit or broken heart can teach you the best lessons in life, especially if you have the support of people who love you. They could be your friends, your coworkers, and sometimes even your family. Enduring pain is hard but know that as long as you still feel pain, it means you are alive. When you make mistakes, you are still human, and know that if you wake up knowing you have the love and support of your loved ones, you still have hope. So, don't let the hope in your heart fade away, and let the fire of love in your spirit kindle. You are not alone, as you have many shoulders to lean on and cry your heart out. Remember, you are awesome. You have a beautiful spirit. So just be you and have a great day.

Good morning, we don't have to be positive all the time. It's perfectly okay to feel sad, angry, annoyed, frustrated, scared, or anxious. Having these feelings or going through a series of emotions doesn't make you a negative person. It is proof of you being human. Don't be afraid and face your challenges head-on. You are an amazing person, never forget that. Allow yourself to share your beautiful spirit with someone and let that 'someone' brighten up your day. Have a fabulous day! Just be you.

Morning, beautiful soul! I know how you feel right now. I know you are overwhelmed; I want you never to forget how far you have come. I want you to remember everything that you have gotten through ever so bravely. I want you to recall all those times when you pushed harder, even when you thought you could not push yourself any further. I want you to remember all those mornings you got out of bed, no matter how hard it was for you. Recall all those times you wanted to give up on that goal but continued to strive towards it, challenging yourself to continue to reach that milestone. Recall the day when you celebrated your triumph upon reaching your goal. I want you never to forget how much strength you had shown to get through those periods or challenges. Remember the skills and attitude that you developed to get you through those times. I want you to know that you are an amazing person, a shining star to so many people. So, just be you and have an awesome day!

When your time on this earth is done, money or material things will not matter, but the love, time, and kindness you have given others will shine and live on forever. Life is very short, so break your silly egos, forgive quickly, believe slowly, love truly, laugh loudly, and never avoid anything that makes you smile or make your belly hurt due to laughing so hard. So, the next time your mind tries to convince you that you can't get through the next difficulty, take a look at all the things you have accomplished so far, the ones that appeared hard but you aced at them. Take a moment to look back at all that you have overcome by believing in yourself. You are great! Just be you and have an awesome day!

Good morning from a lonely moment. On this little journey of mine, I am coming to realize and reflect that anything worth pursuing takes time. The key to my happiness is me, not what other people think. That's why I continue to grow and set new goals and new targets. I am always working on a better version of myself for my own good and my own sake.

In the same way, we all are responsible for our own happiness. So, never stop working on us, and always keep learning. Remember that change is inevitable. It is the one thing we can count on, so embrace it with open arms. One of the most important things I've learned over the years is that our mistakes don't define us, so learn to move past them. My message is important for those who dwell or overthink and sometimes second-guess themselves. Don't ever second-guess yourself. You are awesome! Have a great day, and just be you.

Good morning! My message today is based on a rough day that I had yesterday. I am sorry that I kept it to myself. So many of you are like me. You keep a lot to yourself because it's difficult to find someone who understands you. I want you to be that someone who leaves a mark on people's lives, not scars. I want you to be the one who lifts up the spirits of people and not the one who casts them down for the challenges they face. Be that person who brings out the best in people, not stress them out. Yesterday was a very difficult day for me. My dad, who adopted me, is quite ill. I decided to be that person for him who makes him feel better. I spent the day with him, and it was so amazing that it uplifted my spirit, too. His words made my day. No wonder how good, kind words can do so much to make someone feel good. His three words were, "Hi, my boy!" Those three words were enough to make me feel good. Even though he was not feeling well, he made my day with the smile that he carried on his face. So, remember, you're an awesome human being. Just be you, and have a great day!

Today is a bright and beautiful morning! Life is a mystery, and every day is filled with new lessons. It takes sadness to know what happiness feels like. It takes noise to appreciate silence. And an absence to value presence. I've been away from my boys for five days, and I miss them dearly. At the same time, I appreciate my time off and value all the retrospective thinking I have. Remember you're awesome and that you're a ray of sunshine in someone's life, so just be you. Have a great day!

Rise and shine. Today, I want you to know that happiness is the new measure of success, while health is the new measure of wealth. If you are happy, you are successful. If you are healthy, you are wealthy. Also, kindness is the new cool. The trend today is to be kind and cool. I want you to open your heart and spirit and be like a tree. It always stays rooted firmly in the ground, lets new flowers grow, and the winds sway away old ones, bends before it breaks, and is an integral part of nature. So, be like a tree and enjoy your unique natural beauty and your unique strength of character. Always look forward to what lies ahead of you. Determine your path and keep growing. Remember, you are an amazing person. Just be you, and have a great day!

Good morning! Yesterday was a great day. I had a super evening with a great and dear friend who gave me a challenge and a dare, made her smile and caused a stir on the web, ha-ha. Last night, when I reflected at the end of my day, I realized nothing is more peaceful than a good friend's calm mind, spirit, and heart. Embrace those moments and cherish them. Remembering and honoring them will always get you through a rough patch. Call me crazy, but I love to see other people laugh and succeed. Our lives are our journey, not a competition with the people who don't respect you for who you are. I am glad to find a good friend and role model in you with a kind heart and helpful nature. Enjoy your day, and just be you.

Today is about living by choice, not by chance. Make changes, not excuses. Be motivated, not manipulated, and always work to excel, not to compete. Choose to listen to your inner voice, not the jumbled opinions of everybody else. And make sure you end every day with positive thoughts. No matter how hard things were, today is a new opportunity to make it better. So be the awesome and amazing person that you are and have a great day by just being you!

It's a gorgeous morning! A new day has started here with rain to wash away the sorrow and pain of yesterday. Remember, you will continue to suffer if you focus on the hurt and pain. However, if you focus on the lesson, you will continue to grow, so smile, breathe, and embrace the new day with hope and put your first step forward for today. Remember, you are awesome. Don't forget just to be you.

Good morning! Today is another day, possibly filled with challenges or opportunities. But know that life is going to challenge you every single day. It's not to punish you for your past sins but to train you and give you the strength to push through another day. Trust yourself to make the right choice. Let this be your guide to remain the strong and the amazing person I know you are. Have a great day, and just be you.

Rise and shine, it's morning! Forest Grump once said life is like a box of chocolates, and I couldn't agree more. Every day is different; a perfect life does not exist. So, embrace our imperfections, cherish the lessons, focus on good choices and on the version of you that you can love and celebrate. And that will give you the happy life you desire. Always remember you are a beautiful spirit that makes your people smile when they see you. Have great day and just be you.

Good morning! I hope you slept well and woke up with great energy. From my life's journey, I have learned some interesting lessons, and my spirit tells me that every situation in life is temporary. So, when life is good, make sure you enjoy every moment of it. Most importantly, embrace every event, cherish the moments with the ones you love, and trust those moments fully. Trust me, that's where you get your inner strength from. When life throws challenges at you, remember that's only temporary. Allow your mindset and spirit to think and guide you to the good ahead. Always keep in mind that you're a warrior, your spirit and heart are stronger than you know. Have a great day, and just be you!

Hello, world! The road trip I am doing has been amazing for me and has made me learn a few lessons that I will hold close to my soul. In fact, those lessons have helped me reenergize my spirit. First, let go of things you can't change so you're not a prisoner to them. Always be yourself, stand up for what you believe in, and make sure to question when you are in doubt. Don't have any regrets. Just learn from every experience. Everything happens for a reason, so grow from it. Respect yourself so that you can earn respect from others. Lastly, just do your thing and be awesome. Have a fantastic day and just be you!

It's a new day, and today, I want you to know that your kindness is genuine and not just an act. It reflects the sincerity and honesty of who you are. Your strength isn't solely based on what you can physically do or how much you can handle; it comes from the resilience you've shown in overcoming challenges, even when you thought it was impossible. Sometimes, the scars we carry in our hearts and spirits are not inflicted by enemies but by those who claim to love us. Despite any past hurts, remember that you are strong and possess an incredible heart. So, go ahead and embrace your day with confidence, for you are truly amazing. Be true to yourself. Keep shining, and just be you!

Hello, hello! What a journey it has been, covering many kilometers and sharing wonderful moments with family, including some great belly laughs. Life has a way of revealing who truly matters and who doesn't, and it's an eye-opening experience. You learn to distinguish between fake and true people, as well as those who are always there for you, willing to go the extra mile. Remember, no one changes unless they genuinely want to. It all comes down to making the right moral choices driven by personal decisions. Begging, shaming, reasoning, or tough love won't bring about change unless we realize it ourselves. Don't forget you are awesome. In fact, you are like a ray of sunshine to someone in your life. Have a fantastic day ahead, and remember, just be you!

Let's be grateful as a new day is upon us. Remember, life is short, so let go of negativity and steer clear of gossip and those who don't value your emotions and principles. Spend time with your loved ones and those who bring a smile to your face and genuinely support you when you need it most. Ultimately, what others think of you doesn't matter as much as your own happiness and pride in who you're becoming. What truly counts is being content with yourself and proud of the person you are becoming. Make sure to be in control of your joy and happiness, as you hold the power to validate who you are. So, keep being awesome and amazing. Have a fantastic day ahead, and just be you!

Morning! Say hello to your spirit that always finds the good. When you can't find the sunshine, your spirit guides you to become the sunshine. You have witnessed a level of arrogance and entitlement exhibited by people or leadership that has torn people and communities down instead of uplifting them. They forget leadership is a privilege, but people like you are the ray of sunshine they need to get through the day. You are about great intention and positive behavior, which is your natural practice. Your habit is second nature for you to embrace who you are. It is who you are naturally; the sunshine of many people's lives, the reason people smile and laugh. Remember that you're just a great human being, so just be you!

Hello, hello! Whatever you do today, don't get stuck on the kind of things that may ruin your day. Life is too short to stew on the negativity. One day, you'll look back and realize that you worried too much about things that didn't matter. And in the bigger scheme of things, life is too short. In our lifetime, we do a lot of things. Some we wish we had never done, some we wish we could replay a million times in our head, but these moments make us who we are. They end up shaping every detail about us. Show us how to live, make mistakes, learn, grow, and, most importantly, have great memories. But never ever second-guess who you are, where you have been, and most importantly, where you are going. You are awesome, you are amazing, and you are going to have a great life and remember just be you.

Good morning. I spent the night with my two other rays of sunshine, my daughter and granddaughter. Spending time with my kids always makes me remember why I do what I do. Every morning, we get a new chance to be different, change how we look at things, and respond to negativity more positively. A chance to change, a chance to be better. Your past is in your past. Leave it there. Get on with the future. It is who you are. It is who you are going to be. Being positive doesn't mean you never have negative thoughts. It just means you don't let those thoughts control your life. Remember, you are awesome. You are amazing. Have a great day, and just be you!

Hey, good morning. Let's celebrate today. I used to think I could fix everything in my life if I had given a little bit more time or tried harder. Then, I realized some things are not meant to be fixed. All I can do is make peace with it and share kindness. And move forward. I know I did the best I could with it. And then this hit me: you never know the impact you have on those around you because people always watch and observe you. You could never know how much someone needed that smile you gave them. You never know how your kindness turned someone's entire day around. You never knew how someone needed that deep hug or a long conversation. Don't wait for someone to be kind first. Don't wait for better circumstances or for someone to change everything. Just be kind because you never know when someone needs it. Remember who you are; what you believe is what makes you someone's ray of sunshine, continue to just be you!

Good morning! It took me a while to think of today's message, but I like to think it through. As we shift, grow, and evolve, we get older and wiser. We begin to realize we are not the same people we used to be, the things we used to tolerate. We have now become intolerable. Where we once were quiet, we now speak our truth. Where we once battled and argued, we now choose to stay quiet, listen, and observe. We understand the value of our voices. Some situations and times no longer deserve our time, effort, energy, or focus. So, focus today only on what makes you smile or laugh or puts you in your happy place, in fact just be you!

'Tis a new, beautiful morning! So, take a moment to smile and breathe. Remember to acknowledge all those who came before us, paving the way for our success and triumphs. Every person we encounter teaches us something valuable, some lessons may be painful, while others come effortlessly, but they are all priceless in their own way. Always keep in mind that you are an awesome human being, capable of greatness. Just be yourself and embrace the day with this knowledge, have great day and just be you!

Rise and shine, its morning, and what a day to embrace the realization that everyone has their unique path. Walk your journey with integrity and wish others peace on their way. When paths merge, celebrate their presence in your life, and when they part, return to your own wholeness, grateful for the footprints left in your soul. Now, it's your time to journey on your own. Remember, you are awesome, and to someone, you are like a ray of sunshine. Embrace the day with this positivity. Have a fantastic day ahead and just be you!

Life is about intentional living. Each of us has a purpose in our lives. The most important thing is to care about something. Something that you really like and that makes you feel good. This thing connects to your purpose in life. Find something you love doing, a reason to get up every morning, and keep doing it.

Support the things you believe in, the things that make you special and kind. Have a great day, and just be you!

Many people mention how tough it is to believe in others again after getting hurt. But not many people talk about how tough it is to believe in yourself when someone you trusted and cared for makes you doubt your feelings and thoughts. It's hard to decide when this happens. However, you can choose to look past the bad things. Decide what you want and work for it. Don't forget, you're good, and you're great. I hope you have a wonderful day and just stay true and just be you.

I've talked about making decisions before, so today's message is brief: I've decided not to let bad things ruin the good things in my life anymore. I want to be happy. Remember, you're a wonderful person. It's simple to choose happiness, so go ahead and pick happiness. Have an amazing day and just be you!

I hope you had a good sleep. Just remember, there's nobody else like you in the world. So, let your specialness shine and understand that sometimes our lives need big changes to put us where we truly fit, which is here and now, a peaceful and positive place. You're like a bright light, and that's cool, have great day and just be you!

Good morning! It's nice to smile and say with pride, "I went through tough times but kept moving on in this journey we call life. We learn to handle both good and bad moments, smile even when we're sad, cherish what we have, and remember what we once had. We should forget some things, but we should also remember that people change, and things sometimes don't go right. Still, the important thing is to remember that life keeps moving forward, just like you do. You're like a happy sunbeam, making someone smile and warming their heart when they hear your voice. Have a good day, and just be you!

Today, I realized that we are all special people who become friends in a surprising way. We don't lose good friends, they come into our lives for a good reason, and we should always remember this. It makes me thankful for every moment we have with the people we care about. You've taught me a lot, have an amazing day and just be you!

Good morning! Sometimes, it's tough to move forward after a hard time. But when you decide to move on, you'll see it was a good choice. It all begins with hope and a goal. If you hold onto one thing in your life, let it be hope. Hope reminds you that better days will come. Let hope help you during difficult times. It shows you that you're stronger than any challenge, even in the hardest moments. Hope reminds you that you're where you should be now, and you're on a path to where you're supposed to go. In tough times, hope always helps you. You're great and amazing. Have a pleasant day and just be you!

It's a lovely day, my dear friends! Let me start by saying what I've learned in the past few weeks. Having a calm mind feels peaceful, and having a kind heart is very beautiful. Love your life in a way that makes you smile and feel happy. Life is too short to wake up with regrets. Love the people who treat you well and forget about those who don't. I now believe that everything happens for a reason and has a purpose. So, if you get a chance, take it, and welcome it. Sometimes, things change, and it can be amazing. Just let it happen because life isn't always easy. But trying to be happy and hopeful is worth it. Remember, you are special just the way you are. Have a wonderful day, and just be you!

My thought for today is simple: we often make a big mistake by believing we have a lot of time. I've learned that I don't always need a plan; sometimes, it's enough just to breathe, trust, and let go. See what happens. We can't be sure about tomorrow, so it's good to be thankful every day. Take care of yourself, and appreciate your blessings, like your health, friends, and family. They help you stay hopeful and happy. Make the most of each day because you have a reason and a purpose. Have a wonderful day. Just be you!

I wanted to tell you that you're my friend because you're kind-hearted. Be happy about it and keep it close to you like a special badge. Knowing that to make the world peaceful, we need to find peace inside ourselves. Your smile, your laughter, your company, your positive energy, and your kind heart mean a lot to me. I'm always thankful that you're in my life. Our friendship has a bright future ahead that we haven't experienced yet. So, we'll stick together, stay hopeful, and focus on the good days to come. Be amazing today and just be you!

Good morning! My personal journey so far has taught me some important lessons and changed how I see things. One lesson is that loving yourself brings good things into your life and makes the world better inside and outside. To enjoy what life offers, we need to value ourselves too. Another big lesson for me is that we can't fix bad choices from before, but we have lots of time to make good choices for the future. Sometimes, people who help us believe in miracles and feel hopeful are like every day, angels. They're just like us, have great day and just be you.

Yet another day is here! Just smile and breathe. Why? Because you should always remember how much progress you've made and the tough challenges you've beaten. Think of a butterfly, it shows that there's beauty even after pain. I remember when a window was a hole to see outside, an application was paper for a better future, and a keyboard was on a piano. A mouse was an animal, and a hard drive was an uncomfortable trip. A web was a spider's home, and a virus was like the flu. An apple and a blackberry were just fruits. Those were the days when we had more time for family, friends, creativity, and adventures. So, remember how strong and brave you are. You're a fighter, and you've survived a lot. Celebrate that. The message is simple: Hope is real, don't overthink things. Find what helps you calm the noise and chaos and do it for yourself because you matter! Have great day and just be you.

In a few days, I'll go back to the office, precisely after several weeks of my personal journey of reflection and hope. Here's what I'm thinking about today: I don't have to solve everything right now. I don't need to have all the answers to my problems at this moment. Sometimes, I just need to take a walk or go for a drive without worrying about anything. I can let go of any worries or stress I'm carrying. I shouldn't feel sad or mad. I just want to enjoy the moment, feel happy, and have hope. I want to focus on what really matters to me. I believe that when I do this, my mind, spirit, and body will feel calm, and I'll have positive energy. Reflecting on things is helpful. Just take a deep breath and be okay with who you are. Some people might not like it when you're positive because they prefer it when others are struggling. But your smile can make the world better, so don't let the world change your smile. Our most powerful tool is our ability to think for ourselves. This lets us change things for the better. Remember, you can't change the past, but you can start now and make a better future. Embrace today and just be you!

Good morning! I'm sorry I didn't get time yesterday to write down my thoughts. I was busy herding cattle on a horse, and later, I needed to rest because my body was tired from riding. While on the horse, I thought about how many people don't fully appreciate life. The past three weeks have helped me see the value in small things. When something big happens, it makes us think about our purpose in life and why we do what we do. Catastrophes, illness, and death teach us important lessons and make us more aware of ourselves. I've realized that our struggles give us a chance to grow and learn. These tough moments in life are like steps that lead us to a better understanding. Life gives us these lessons as temporary gifts that we should appreciate. Sometimes, we don't learn quickly, so life keeps giving us challenges to wake us up and make us think about how we're living. The ups and downs in life show us that anything can happen, and we need to embrace that. Life and time let us learn, find our talents, and contribute to making our world better. So, take some time to think and learn. Just be you and live your life to the fullest.

We all reach a point where we need to make a choice: stay the same or grow. If you stay the same, you'll face the same challenges, routines, storms, and situations until you learn from them. When you truly care about yourself, you'll say, "no more" and choose change. If you choose to grow, you'll find the strength within you. You'll be open to exploring beyond your comfort zone. You'll wake up each morning loving yourself. You'll become who you're meant to be. You already have what you need inside you. Decide to grow, choose love, and believe in your strength. Have great day and just be you.

Good morning! Someone once told me that happiness can be a stranger, coming and going. After my travels in the past few weeks, here's what I think about that idea: Happiness changes. What makes you happy today might not be the same tomorrow. The things that excite you in the future could be different. Our happiness depends on how we feel in the present. Happiness comes to us in various ways to satisfy what we're looking for. It might come through an object, a person, or the realization of a dream we've been chasing. Whenever it arrives, it's at the right time. Maybe it's destiny. I'm not sure. So, dream big, pursue your dreams, find contentment, and have a great day. Don't forget to just be you!

It is a great morning! Start your day with a smile, take a deep breath, and acknowledge all those who've paved the way for your success and triumphs. Life teaches us valuable lessons through everyone who crosses our path, some may be tough, while others come easily, but each is truly priceless. Always remember that you are an extraordinary human being. Don't forget just to be you.

It's an amazing day to realize that everyone has their unique path in life. Walk yours with integrity and extend well wishes for peace to everyone on their journeys. When your paths cross, celebrate the joy of their presence in your life. And when they go in different directions, return to your inner wholeness and be grateful for the footprints they've left in your soul. Don't forget to embrace the opportunity to continue your journey on your own. Always remember that you are an amazing individual and a ray of sunshine to someone out there. Have a fantastic day, and just be you!

Good morning! Life is all about intentional living. Every individual has a unique purpose, and how we choose to fulfill it is in our hands. What's crucial is having a cause that ignites our spirit and connects us to our life's purpose. Find that purpose, a reason to wake up every day, and stand up for what you believe in. You're an awesome, unique, and good-hearted individual. Have a great day, and just be you!

It's such a beautiful day! Trusting yourself can be just as challenging as trusting others after being hurt. When someone you trust undermines your instincts and convictions, it can shake your self-confidence. The real challenge lies in choosing to move beyond negativity, setting your goals, and pursuing them. Always remember, you are awesome and amazing, capable of overcoming these challenges. Just be you and enjoy your day.

Morning, rise and shine! I have spoken about choice before, so here's a short message: I choose not to let negativity overshadow the good in our lives. I've chosen happiness. Remember, you're amazing. Choosing happiness is simple. Wishing you a fantastic day and be yourself!

It's a lovely day, my dear ones. I hope you slept well. Remember, there is no one else in the world like you. Shine your unique light and know that sometimes life needs to shake up to place us where we belong in a peaceful and positive place. You're an amazing ray of light. Have a wonderful day, and just be you!

A new day is upon us. It's a beautiful thing to smile and proudly say, "I fell apart and kept going on this road we call life." We learn to embrace both the good and the bad, smile through sadness, cherish what we have, and hold onto our memories. People change, things go wrong, but remember, your choice is to keep going. You are the ray of sunshine, the one who makes someone smile and warms their heart with your voice. Always be yourself, have a great day and just be you!

Good morning! Today, I recognize you are someone special who has entered my life. You entered it unexpectedly as a friend, and I won't let you go. You've come into my life for a reason, a reason I deeply cherish. You've taught me the value of appreciating every moment with those we love and how precious life truly is. Thank you for being such an amazing friend. Have a fantastic day, and just be you!

It's a new day! Moving on after tough times can be challenging, but it often turns out to be the best decision. It all begins with hope and a goal. If you carry one thing throughout your life, let it be hope. That is because hope reminds you that better days are ahead, that you're stronger than any challenge, and that you're where you're meant to be on your journey. In tough times, it is important to remember that hope belongs to you and that hope will carry you through during tough times. You're awesome and amazing. Have a wonderful day, and just be you!

Good morning! I want you to know that you are my friend because of your kind heart, and I'm proud of that. Embrace your kindness like a badge of honor. Peace in the world starts with discovering peace within yourself, and your smile, laughter, presence, spirit, and kind heart contribute to that. I'm grateful for your part in my life, and I believe our friendship holds a bright future we've yet to see. Together, we'll rise with hope, always looking ahead to brighter days. Thanks for being my friend. Enjoy your day and stay true to yourself, and just be you!

It is a bright and beautiful morning, so just remember to smile and breathe. Why? Because you should never forget how far you've come and the personal challenges you've overcome. Like a butterfly emerging from a cocoon, beauty often follows pain. You've come a long way, and you're a fighter and survivor. Celebrate that. The essence of this message is simple: hope exists. Don't overthink. Find what brings peace amidst the noise, clear your chaos, and just be you. Have a fantastic day.

It's a new day, so just breathe, accept who you are, and be a positive influence in this negative world. Being a positive person offends those who thrive on negativity. So let your smile change the world, but don't let the world change your smile. Because the most powerful tool we have is our positive thinking which allows us to change any situation. And since we can't fix our past, we can always start fresh. With this said, have a great day, and just be you!

It's my first day back to work after almost a month and a half, and I have realized that people have different definitions of courage. Courage doesn't mean diving head-first on ground zero. It means we hold our own and prevent fear from getting in the way of our dreams. So, power through today, be courageous and follow your heart to where it takes you. Have a great day and just be you!

Good afternoon! Today's message took some reflection. I want to begin by emphasizing that standing alone doesn't mean I am alone; it, in fact, means I am strong enough to handle things independently. Moreover, perhaps we all have the power to transform our lives into remarkable stories when we view difficulties as opportunities. Sometimes, our lives need a significant shake-up, a change, or a rearrangement to guide us to where we truly belong or are meant to be. Stay focused, be courageous, and have a wonderful day, and just be you!

It is a beautiful morning! Ensure your choices align with your hopes and not your fears. A single disappointment, a bad day, a poor decision, or a failed relationship does not define you. You are more than setbacks and mistakes. Learn from them and become a better version of yourself. By choosing happiness, you are steering your life in a positive direction. Have faith in yourself. Have a wonderful day, and always just be you!

There's nothing in this world that can trouble us more than our own thoughts. There's too much ahead of us in life, and life is a beautiful thing to waste on things that don't matter. Live your life your way and write every chapter so you can turn the page to see what happens next, always in a positive light. Follow your dreams and love yourself deeply. Be happy, don't judge, celebrate every moment of becoming you, and be true to yourself. Take every step that takes you to the point of your joy and happiness and makes you feel better than you did before. Have an amazing day, and just be you.

Good morning. Hope this morning finds you in good spirits, with the same kind heart you went to bed with. Continue to be the person you are. I have learned not to pretend to be anything other than me or anything that I'm not. I am kind, I am loyal, I always have the back of those close to me and my friends, and I stand by what I believe in. I'm not professing to be perfect. I am just the most authentic version of myself. So today, be kind, loyal, and authentic. I know that's who you are. Have a great day, and just be you.

I just wanted you to know and remind you, you are amazing, strong, talented, and have a beautiful spirit. And remember, you are not alone on this crazy journey of life. Lean on those you depend on and those who depend on you. I am here to walk with you always. Have a great journey and just be you!

This morning, I woke up with a clear reminder to say thank you to all the special people in my life. Those who listen without judgment, who have helped without conditions, who understood with empathy, loved, and supported me no matter what. So, because of all of you, I think positive thoughts every morning. I think big, I think healing, I think inner peace, I think success, I think with a growth mindset, and most importantly, I think happiness. Always start every day with positive energy and positive thoughts. We all deserve it. You're in my circle. Have a great day, and just be you.

It's a beautiful day to remember that you don't need a new day to start over; you only need a positive mindset every morning and every night. Happiness is not something you postpone for the future; it is something your mind and heart design for the present. Everything comes to you at the right moment; be patient. So, look back and be grateful, look ahead and be hopeful, and today, look around and be helpful. Because remember, never underestimate yourself; you are better than you think. Just be you!

Good morning. I hope today finds you with a smile, looking out into the sunshine, and a soul filled with hope and big dreams. I had a big awakening this morning as I came to a crossroads in my life, a point of growth and realization. I realize that not everybody changes. Some people never change and really don't want to change. Their journey is not our responsibility, and it does not include us trying to fix them if they are broken in our eyes. Because we learn nothing if we believe we are always right, especially when it comes to other people, their behaviors, their attitudes, and their perceived gaps according to us. So, we must learn not to let our emotions take over our intelligence in guiding our paths. How they treat us is usually an indication of how they feel about us. So today, be your own ray of sunshine. Have a great day, and just be you!

Good morning. I hope today finds you with a glimmer of hope and aspiring attainable dreams. Nothing is more peaceful than a calm mind and more beautiful than a kind heart. Some people call me crazy and sometimes silly, but I love to see people happy and succeeding. I must remind myself and my kids that life is a journey full of challenges and successes, not a competition. Be patient, tolerant, and supportive, and you will reap what you sow. So, have an awesome day, and just be you.

Here's a simple message for this morning: just claim your worth, love your life, and believe in your dreams. Be grateful for this day. Remember, sometimes you need to take steps alone to discover your path and your true self. Free yourself from the weight of past mistakes and forgive yourself for what you've been through. Every day, life gives you the opportunity to start anew. Set goals, speak your dreams aloud, and make choices that are right for you. Have a great day, and just be you!

Good morning. Good things come to those who have hope and believe, better things come to those who are patient and resourceful, and the best things come to those who don't give up and see the opportunity of challenges. Just be awesome. Have a great day, and don't forget to just be you.

Take life day by day and be grateful for the little things. Don't get stressed about the things you can't control. When you choose to face your fears, you take away their power. So, all we should deal with in challenging times is one day or one thing at a time. We can't go back to yesterday, and we can't control tomorrow, so embrace every moment today. Cherish the choices you make for yourself because you are a beautiful spirit cherished by many. Have a great day, and just be you.

Another morning of calm reflection. It's funny how we outgrow the things we once thought we couldn't live without and then fall in love with the things, we didn't even know we wanted. Life just keeps leading us on these journeys we would've never gone on if it was up to us. Don't be afraid, have faith, find the lessons, and enjoy the journey. Trust your path. I reflect on this as I sit in a hotel lobby and see Ukrainian families check into the hotel after leaving everything that they've known and built, to start over with very little that takes real courage and hope. Don't take the days for granted. Breathe, embrace, and cherish. Just be you!

Good morning. I share a sad but amazing morning with you today. Don't go through life. Grow through life. Appreciate where you are in your journey; it serves your purpose, even if it's not where you want to be. Every season has its purpose, and when you least expect it, something awesome will come along, something better than you ever planned for. So be patient, be smart, and stay focused. Just dance till the music is over. Live the best version of you. You are a bright star in the evening sky. Have a great day, and just be you.

Hello, sunshine! While everyone wants to be the sunshine in people's lives, sometimes you need to be the moon that shines in their darkest hours. Be that bright star, and never stop believing in what you want to do. Remember, the person with big dreams is more powerful than the one with all the facts. Use the facts to realize your dreams. Be amazing, be awesome. Have a great day, and just be you.

Good morning! It has been quite a morning indeed. Remember, regret can't change the past, and anxiety won't change the future. However, gratitude has the power to transform the present. Learn to create your own happiness, and no one can take it from you. Sometimes, unexpected blessings come when you least expect them. So, be patient, tolerant, respectful, and positive. Remove negativity from your thoughts and energy. We are all awesome and amazing people with good, and kind hearts. Have a fantastic day, and always be yourself! Have a great day, and just be you.

It's a wonderful day, and it's great to hear that you woke up with a new positive outlook and direction. Every morning, we should remind ourselves that, no matter how tough it may be, "I am going to make it." Remember, making yourself a priority is not selfish; it's necessary. We can't always control the circumstances, but we can control how we react to them. Managing our attitude and directing positive efforts and energy can make a world of difference. Just be you!

Rise and shine! After a hectic week, it's important to remember that we spend most of our lives inside our heads, so let's make it a nice place to be. Sometimes, it might feel like we're losing control, but hope is the key to maintaining a positive outlook. Think of maple and oak trees; they display vibrant colors before shedding their leaves and endure harsh winters, patiently waiting for warmer weather to grow new leaves. Like the maple tree's sap that becomes maple syrup, we, too, can transform challenges into something sweet. So, stand tall, brighten the day with your colorful presence, and have a great day. Always just be you!

Good morning, my friend. Embrace that moment when you realize you're not the person you used to be. You're no longer the person of pain and trauma. You are the person of choice and hope. Life has changed us. The old you has slowly faded away into the fabric of the past. Cherish the hope and dreams not yet realized. No need to feel the scars of the past because they no longer cause you pain and suffering. They are now simply a part of your story to embrace and share, to give hope, and to inspire others to dream. Because the scars are no longer something we run from because they became the thing that gave us the strength of who we are right now an awesome, amazing human being with a good heart and shining spirit. Have a great day, and just be you.

Closing end-of-week thoughts for you and your weekend: You may not always see the results of your kindness or the ray of sunshine and hope you spread around you and to the people who matter to you. So go into the weekend knowing that every bit of kindness and positive energy that you shared and contributed to the world this week surely made the world a better place for us all. Have a great weekend and just be you.

Good morning. My spirit has been freed to share daily positive energy with my friends, with the idea that every morning we say thank you, and may every sunrise bring us hope and every sunset give us peace. Because sometimes in life, we just need a hug, a kind word, no advice, just a hug followed by a kind word. So enjoy my virtual hug, have great day and just be you.

Hello, a new day for new insight. The more we focus on what we want in life, where we want to be, and who we want to be, the faster it will become our reality. Like dreams become creeks, and creeks become mighty rivers, hope is a very small word grounded in the idea of great potential. So, with a combination of focus and hope, embrace today. Have a great day, and just be you!

I hope today finds you in good spirits and positive energy. I've spent the last couple of days in deep reflection. Every now and then, someone enters our lives with no agenda, no ulterior motive, and no self-interest but who takes pleasure in helping guide us to grow, succeed, and find and live our purpose. This person operates with honor and respect and seeks no praise or anything in return. This person has been a gift. So, work hard, listen more attentively, talk less, do what you know is right, learn from your mistakes, build people up, laugh often, stop complaining, and invest in yourself. Reflect, plan, dream big, and, most importantly, love unconditionally. We all need guidance and support. Have a great day, and just be you.

Good morning, my friend. Today is a new day full of hope and new pursuits to build our inner strength. Trust me, if you've been hurt many times and are still able to smile or cry openly, you are strong. Believe me, all our sacrifices and silent cries will pay off, supported by your ability to trust and embrace hope. Never apologize for being emotional and sensitive; it's a sign that you have a good heart, believe in the goodness of the world, and are not afraid to let other people see it. Showing your emotions and vulnerability is a sign of your strength. Ask for what you want in life, take risks, and don't be afraid of failure. You will never realize your dreams if you don't pursue them. As Nike says, 'Just do it'. Trust and believe that.

Good day to you. I hope this morning brings immense happiness and tranquility to your life. Among so many powerful messages, remember that in life, there will be times when we all find ourselves on the verge of collapsing. When we see things slipping away and find it tough to put things in perspective, in that moment, we must stay true to our belief and the power given to us by a higher power. Only then will we be able to make it through such tough situations? Sometimes, we should let things be as they are and wait for them to make sense. Until then, be patient and resilient to new beginnings, and don't forget to embrace the true you. Never lose yourself in chaos. In fact, the brave are those who find themselves in the dark and learn to rise above their circumstances. Have a great day, and just be you!

Good morning! Life is indeed challenging to those who don't know its real mantra. Sometimes, it's a garden full of roses, and sometimes, it's full of thorns. The tough experience of letting our loved ones, who we want to spend our life with, go was only a one chapter in our story. The experience is tough, but this is how the world operates. Wise are those who welcome the change and accept the harsh realities; they move on with what life offers, keeping pure intentions for others. We all need to realize that this life is a journey, which allows us to grow and evolve. So, it's always great to accept the better and improved version of ourselves who has remained poised and steadfast throughout the process. I am proud of who you are and how far you have come with your self-belief and wisdom. Just be you.

More power to you. Wishing you a great day ahead! On an amazing morning, let me remind you of the powerful message where you must set your own precedent. Indeed, you have written your story, but it's up to you how well you articulate it to the world. Never let anyone dictate your life, always take charge of your actions, and exhibit the best in you. Your life stories, especially your past, are what transform you majorly; never give anyone a chance to play with your feelings. Pull yourself together in the worst of scenarios and stand tall with your morals and character. Always choose to grow instead of being stagnant, learn new things, and allow change in life. With all this, I wish you all the very best, and cheers to new beginnings. Have a great day and just be you!

Hello, hello! Today embarks a new day to a new beginning today is the day of celebration to make it to the new you successfully. I truly believe that beautiful things will happen when we distance ourselves from negativities, when we surround ourselves with hope and positivity, and when we vow to learn new lessons. When we say goodbye to unrealistic challenges and unleash our potential to sew a wider horizon of life, we should never lose our true selves in competition with others. Instead, allow yourself to make new friends, and learn the art of companionship, honor the gifts you have been given to you, and just be you.

Greetings! Today is the day to look out at the new offerings' life has for us. Today, we will look at ourselves beyond where we usually see. Today is the day when we won't miss out on any chance. Today can be a turning point in your life when you will find yourself on the top. This is the path forward towards your bright future. The past experiences that helped you shape your real self are the major contribution to making you tough and headstrong. Make wise choices and stick to the decision you take because you know what is best for you. Always remember to just be you.

Good morning! On this day, we will look at the brighter side of life, where we will take a step forward and leave our past. We will progress to creating a safer space for ourselves, we will value our feelings and prioritize peace and happiness. We will learn the art of leaving the bad memories and holding on to the moments that keep us cherished and joyous. For the bad days, we will learn to survive and be hopeful for the better days, as nothing lasts forever. Have a beautiful day, and just be you.

Morning sunshine! On this day, we will learn to stay calm and quiet. Sometimes, all you need is to resonate with your own thoughts. For this day, we will learn to remain poised, where we won't respond to the chaos, and be ourselves with a strong faith in our higher power. This day will be a symbol of peace and triumph, it will exhibit our true self. Remember, you are beautiful, and you deserve to be happy. It's time to keep your head high and move on with life. Never chase anyone, and never let yourself down in the process. Just be you.

Good morning. On this day, we will forgive ourselves for the mistakes we made in our past. We will be kind to ourselves and accept our flaws. Today, we will choose to continue walking on the path that keeps us happy and content; today, we will learn to make progress. No matter how small of a contribution we make, we will prioritize learning new things and being our true selves. On this day, we will eliminate the elements that block our happiness, and we will add newness to life in terms of better health and new and improved habits. Today, we vow never to look back and create new possibilities for a better and brighter tomorrow. Believe in yourself, and just be you.

Good day! A beautiful day begins with a beautiful mindset. When you wake up in the morning, take a deep breath and consider the privilege of being alive and healthy. Happier moments await us, but to reach them, we must embrace the challenge of letting go of things we are unable to change. Moving on can be tough, but once you do, you'll realize it was the best decision for yourself. Remember, if you can see it and believe it, you can achieve it. Just be you.

I'm thankful for today as I've been reflecting on the events of the past, and it has filled me with new hope. Life can change in the blink of an eye. I'd rather face daily struggles, building on my strengths and holding fast to my hopes and dreams, than give someone the power to claim credit for my journey. It might be too late to change the past or the choices I thought were bad, but there's ample time to make the right choices for the future. Be guided by hope, your inner strength, find your peace, and believe in yourself. Embrace happiness and just be you.

Good morning! Welcome your day with joy and hope in life. There are times when we make our own choices that give us joy and pave our way for the future. Never miss out on those precious moments; make memories that help you to hold on to them. As your past can never come back, fill your present with bliss, and most importantly, recognize the real you. Don't fake yourself around people; instead, teach them the art of being themselves. At the end of the day, what matters is you, so just be yourself and don't lose yourself in the process. Just be you!

Good morning, friends! In the world of competition today, we choose to be loyal and grateful for the blessings we take for granted. We will take an exit from the rat race and be humble towards our souls. As I sit at the airport to attend my adopted dad's funeral, I recall how lucky it is to be in a healthy state. Time never comes back so value your present and live it to the fullest. Have a great day, and just be you.

Great morning, buddies; as I reflect, I realize the importance of memories. In today's fast-paced world, we have forgotten the art of creating memories. They are the essence of living through, the memories that keep you going and help you recall the precious stages of your life. These memories are the cornerstone to push you through. Memories are precious, they are the guiding path to your journey ahead. The memories remind us of our loved ones, the ones who care for us, the ones who were with us through thick and thin. Hold on to your lively past and learn to live the incredible present. Have a great day, and just be you.

Good morning! On this day, we will make time to remember the precious souls who made an impact in our lives and who made our lives loving and memorable. Those who hold a special place in our hearts, without whom we would not be able to achieve our goals. Today is a day to celebrate and cherish moments with the people who believe in you. There are ones who teach us great life lessons, the art of being happy and persistent. The major blessing is to have sincere and loyal people around you; such people are gems, value them the most. Live your life to the fullest and just be you.

Good morning, fellows; as I sit in my sister's house beside my dad's ashes, I reflect on the idea of what he and I would be talking about right now or the notion that someday this will all make sense. Throughout my life, I have learned some profound lessons, out of which was to put things in perspective. There will be days in your life that will make you feel low on energy but, friends in that confusion and darkness, don't lose hope. Always believe the idea that you can never connect the dots looking forward, but there comes a time in life when everything that didn't fall in place will feel complete and wholesome. Your efforts will not be wasted, and you will be satisfied. Learn to shine in all circumstances. Have a great day, and just be you.

Good day! So, friends, today, we will highlight a great lesson about how your company of people shapes you. We often underestimate the power of the company; we overlook the fact that the people around you play a vital role in forming your perspective and your personality. Keeping this idea in mind, I try to surround myself with positive people who strengthen my faith, stand by me, and give me a wider perspective on life. Believe me, it has helped me immensely reconstruct my notion of positivity, growth, and success. Whenever I start to fall short on belief and motivation, my people back me, and I find myself stronger than before, and that's the real power of wise company. It has brought about a great change in my life, and I notice that things have changed for me. With this stay strong, stay hopeful, believe in yourself, have a great day, and don't forget just to be you.

Hello friends! Today's lesson will teach you the art of living in the moment. Many times, in life, you will experience the harsh realities. Those harsh realities are not to let you down, instead, they are there to polish you. After a few weeks of deep reflection, sometimes we must let go of the picture in our head of what we thought of life. There will be things that will make us feel down, but remember, there will be things that will remind us to be grateful for. Never ignore the blessing of health, our ability to think, respond, and overcome life's challenges. Life happens, people happen, but never avoid the power that has been gifted to you. Stay strong and have a great day, don't lose the true essence of life, just be you.

Good morning! As I look up at the wider horizon, I find nothing but the vastness of the universe. When life treats you badly, you don't have to react the same way. Remember your brain is a great ruling organ, whatever you feed into your brain, it happens to come back. Keeping this idea in mind, always believe in your powers and abilities. Learn to find hope in the dark tunnel; believe me, friends, it works like magic. It will boost your belief in positivity, and you will see good things coming your way. Letting go of what you perceive to be your dark past is the best choice one can make, as it opens new pathways, empowers you in different ways, and makes you realize your true motive in this world. Sometimes, the smallest step forward in the right direction ends up being the biggest step in your life, so tiptoe if you must but take the step. Have a great day, and just be you.

Good day! Hope you are living your life very beautifully. Today, I am sharing a powerful message with you guys, and it is self-acceptance. It might sound challenging but believe me when you learn this art, it will feel so peaceful and needed. It will free us from unnecessary doubts, and you will find yourself at ease. That feeling of being indifferent to the world is powerful enough to get you through the storms of life. Social norms drive us to be someone else that we are not in reality. We are all unique and awesome in our own way, and we need to tell it to the world by shouting out loud. It can only be done when we become unapologetically ourselves and embrace who we really are. When we no longer get intimidated by the idea of what people think of us, that is the state when we start looking beyond our flaws and our doubts of the past. Remember this powerful message and just be you.

Good morning! It's crazy because today I realized that I am on my new journey, a new chapter of life, and I need to trust the magic of this next chapter. Change is not easy, but it's all that you need at times. Don't hassle to get into the change, don't rush into doing the things right away. Take one step at a time; sometimes, we fancy the idea of getting things done right away and having the results, but it's not how it works. Always believe that people with good hearts always get good in return; you will be astonished to see how nicely it will work in your favor. It might feel overwhelming to achieve your goal and be good to people at the same time but take a deep breath and continue on the wonderful journey of achieving, you will see wonders happening around you. Have a great day, and just be you.

Rise and shine! Not everyone will have the heart that you have, so this morning, celebrate the goodness in you, the motivation that you live through. Not everyone will appreciate you and your acts, so be kind to yourself, appreciate yourself, and be patient with what people say about you. Believe that you are truly blessed. Your kindness can be the reason to live for many. All you need to have been a firm belief in the good things. Treat yourself better and see goodness making its way to you. Cherish your present, have a good day, and just be you.

Good morning! Today you need to value what you really have; you need to appreciate the things around you. You need to gain the energy that keeps you going. Value yourself and uplift your spirit that allows you to work beyond the horizon. Don't listen to those who undervalue the real you. The best you can do is to spread the positivity that reflects. Have a great day, and just be you.

Good day! Being positive is the true essence of life one can have. In the beginning, it might sound daunting to stay positive and firm in your belief. But remember dirty water doesn't prevent plants from growing. So, continue your positive path, and you will see miracles happening for you. Progress requires you to look forward to and welcome the great things. Whatever you are stressing about today will not matter tomorrow, so breathe, embrace, and cherish the blessings that you have. Wishing you a great day ahead and just be you.

Good morning! Today, we will celebrate the new us, the journey that shaped us into becoming who we really are. On this day, we will remember the milestones that we have achieved over time. The goals seemed unattainable in the beginning, but our faith in us led us here. We are proud and thankful for how far we have come and how far we have to go. Today embarks on the day of success when we will cherish our strengths and move on with life. Have a great day, and as always, just be you.

Hello, my friends! On this day, we vow to set the precedent of hard work and self-belief, where we will remain committed to the goal we have set for ourselves. We will be thankful for what we have today and work hard for what we want for tomorrow. With this, I wish you a great day ahead, and remember to just to be you.

Good morning! Many times, in life, we feel like things are falling apart, but in reality, they are falling into place. So, remember to use your voice for kindness, your ears for compassion, your hands for charity, your mind for truth, and, of course, your heart for love. Have a great day, and just be you.

Rise and shine! May this day bring you immense joy and happiness. If we spend years reliving our experiences from the past, we also need to give ourselves permission to remember without reliving it. It's okay to experience peace and joy. Today, we must be careful that we don't let the circumstances of our lives take a toll on us. Life is the name of experiences; let your experiences never make you feel down, move on with a belief to heal as time is the best healer. We always have the choice to move forward, seek happiness and joy, find good, and be free. Have a great day, and just be you.

Good morning, my people! Always remember, choice is that one thing that always lingers because it takes a certain period to polish you and transform you into your greatest. Sometimes, you will have to make tough choices, and you will feel bad about them but don't blame yourself for your feelings. Give yourself some time, go to places and live to your fullest. Surround yourself with the people who are good and supportive of you. Believe in yourself and share an honest laugh, an honest conversation of issues during those moments. You'll be remembered more for your kindness than any level of success you could possibly attain. In the journey, you will find some people who are so kind to you, it's because the world has been so unkind to them, they underwent the misery of not being loved and understood. With a little bit of kindness and love, we can spread positivity and be a reason to someone's smile. Remember to be happy, and always, just be you!

Good morning, my friends! The hardest test in life is patience and waiting for your moment. There will be moments in your life when you'll feel devastated and hollow, but in that moment, you must stand and gather your courage to stay kind to yourself. Some people forget themselves in the process, they forget who they really are and their real motive in this world. Sometimes, letting go of the burden is the best way out to release yourself from the worries. You will get to see many ups and downs, but what you should never lose at all cost, are the true and sincere friends. The friends who'll never let you down, who back you in times of need. So, stay focused and use the past as lessons to shape your future. You deserve to be happy and content. Have a great day and remember to be true and humble. Just be you.

Good day! Today, instead of focusing on all the things that are going wrong, we will learn to be thankful for all the things and blessings sent our way. There are times, when we get lost in the present, when we forget to be happy and grateful. Remember, being grateful is one step to being happy and as you move ahead, you will realize that nothing or no one really matters when you learn to trust yourself and your plans. Your ability to see, smell, laugh, cry, and understand is a great blessing. Surround yourself with beautiful and positive people who believe in you. Because in the blink of an eye, everything can change. So, forgive often love with all your heart. Remember you can only spread happiness, positivity and wisdom if you have it for you. Because it's impossible to give what you don't have, so be kind to yourself, discover who you really are, and wait for the things to fall in place. Have a great day and just be you.

Hello my people! Today I want you to venture into a new direction or beginning, which is both scary and exciting. The last 7 weeks challenged me outside of my comfort zone, so I embraced this new beginning, the best part of this whole thing is I didn't wait for a perfect moment to begin a new chapter of life. This new chapter is a perfect start of my life. It gave me courage to determine what is to come in my life ahead, it helped me strengthen my inner self. Sometimes, change is mandatory for a new beginning, it's important to keep moving and have a motivation in life. Cherish and embrace the new you. Have a great day and just be you.

Good morning! We will start today with a positive mindset, as it is the key to being happy. The positive mindset is knowing that you have the power to choose, accept, and move on. Don't wait for an ideal condition or time, as what to accept and what to let go don't wait for the perfect time. The foremost step to the new beginnings is to believe and move on. You can declutter yourself from the worries and anxiety that really bothers you. Breathe in the open air, allow happiness to chase you and remain content. With this lesson, I wish you best of luck and just be you.

Look alive! Wake up and smile today with a shine in your eyes, relieve yourself from the worries, and treat yourself in the best way possible. Today, we'll start our day with a beautiful spirit, and positive mindset. As life is a journey full of problems, but the main aim of the wise people is to hold on to their ability to remain unbeatable, and unapologetically great. We need to learn the art to solve lessons, to mend and hope living its greatest journey but most of all experience we need to enjoy the process. It's not the destination that makes you happy, it's the journey and process that shape you as an individual. So, be patient, trust what is to come, and just be you.

Good day my people! Today we will talk about wisdom, we will highlight how your wise decisions and choices will pave your way to success. In the world full of people, you will find many who don't possess the ability to choose for themselves. They decide on what others think of them and continue their journey on others' judgement. In this process, they lose their ability to learn, and succeed. Following what others do never helps until it really works in your favor, never chase the thing or person who does not feel peaceful at all, instead, learn to be happy and follow your dreams with a positive approach. When you vow to bring a change in the world, always be mindful of the fact that the process of bringing change will require you to stay firm, no matter what the circumstances are. Never lose your true self and keep working hard. Embrace the idea that failure is a part of creating a good life, embrace the moments of despair, cherish the moments of acknowledgements, smile breathe and be happy. Have a great day and just be you

Good morning! This day, we reflect back to our powers and strengths that differentiate us from others. This day, we decide to be our strengths who don't need anyone's support, this day we vow to be self-sufficient and self-reliant. We are smarter because of our mistakes, and the lessons we have learned throughout our journey. We know how to cherish the moments of happiness because we have experienced sadness, we have been through the rough phase of our lives that taught us to remain happy in our present. We are wiser and more patient because of all of those lessons. It's our choice to opt for change or be stagnant. Wise people always opt for change that can bring them harmony and inner peace. So go for it today, no matter how it goes, at the end of the day, it's the experience that matters. Have a great day and just be you.

Good morning, my friends! This lesson is about the profound learning experience that comes when we try to attain our goals. Dreams are not easy to fulfill, but the true commitment makes the journey worthwhile. Enjoying our journey and remaining true to our dreams is an art that is known by very few. Many people give up in the process as they lack guidance and clarity and this is where the real struggle starts. When you give up on your dreams, we become perplexed as to where to go now, this is the time when negativities attack us, make us feel vulnerable. Many tend to lose their actual personalities, and the overwhelming circumstances come crashing down on us. Therefore, the journey might feel tough but remember, the tougher the journey, the sweeter the fruit. In the times of hardship, recall the sentence, "this too shall pass" and learn from the past experiences to avoid the mistakes in future. Embrace the new day as a new beginning, look beyond the horizon and just be you.

Good day! The power of the mind and the heart are what truly makes us who we are. Only we know our heart and the feelings associated with it. The desire to reach somewhere and change your dreams into reality is what truly matters. My friends, only we know what we truly want and only we can make the things work in our favor. You can clutch onto the past so tightly to your chest allowing us to embrace, and hold onto the present. Be proud of your success and the journey you have come through. Life is too short to hold on to misfortune and mishaps. Time is precious, so hold on to it, make the most of your present. Have a great day ahead and just be you.

Good morning! Today we'll focus on how to train your mind to look at the positive output. Today, your mind will tell you a lot of things, today your soul will question your heart and your actions but you have to stay calm and composed. There are times in life, when we question our practices, when we feel useless, when unnecessary questions arise and divert our focus. In those tough moments, learn to be you, learn to shun those thoughts, take a break, and avoid overwhelming feelings. Prioritize your peace, trust your heart. With this I wish you a great day ahead, and just be you.

Good morning my friend! Sometimes, we are so tired that we don't know who we are. This past year, I realized two types of tired people, one that requires rest and one that requires peace, I chose peace. Sometimes the best thing we can do is to let go of our worries. Don't think the worst, nor fascinate the best, just be in present and focus on what is required. Sometimes, we just need to sit back, breathe and have faith that everything will work in the best way possible. In our constant rush to return to normal, we lose time to reflect and consider which parts of our soul are worth rushing back to. Choose your peace, choose your state and keep going. Have an amazing day and just be you.

Good day! In reflection of choices on life lessons, always keep in mind that you're never too old to set a new goal or to dream. I know the storm of confusion and self-doubt will not let you sit in peace but keep in mind that this too shall pass, soon we will see clear sunny skies again directing us to a positive path forward. Be grateful for the people in our lives that contributed to shaping our personalities, who trusted us and supported us through our thick and our thin. Be thankful for the new day and a new chance that calls for a new beginning. Have a great day and just be you

Good morning! Today I will drive you through my experience and the words of wisdom that my elders used to share with me. I remember being told by my grandparents and elders that our mind and spirits will always believe what we tell them. So, feed it with truth, happiness, love and compassion. We underestimate the power of a smile, a kind word, a listening ear and an honest compliment. Sometimes, the smallest act of kindness or caring of the small gestures have the potential to create a change to someone's life. Sometimes, we need to be quiet to make peace with the battles inside us to sort out the chaos. That time requires us to filter all of our negative thoughts and seek the positivity and comfort. Always remember, every dark chapter is followed by a brighter one so train your mind to be patient in order to get the best outcomes after every trial. Look forward to the new beginnings, breathe and cherish all that you have. Have a great day and once again, just be you

Happy sunshine! Embrace this new day filled with new challenges to make a difference to your life. Understand that perfection is not everything, you can't be perfect at all times, sometimes the best in you is the imperfection that makes you stand out in the crowd. Free yourself from the worldly parameters of beauty, life, wealth and success, just embrace where you come from and this time, be unapologetically you and have a great day, and just be you.

Good day! On this chilly and wintry morning, you're meant to take a fresh start. It's the practice that I follow that has helped me transform who I really am. That teaching is to be always happy and contentment, especially when you see the things slipping away from our hands. Get a hold of ourselves and react to each situation wisely. I have seen people working immensely hard to reach their goal, all they are concerned with is to reach the mountaintop. But, when they reach there, they don't feel happy at all. Have you ever wondered, why? It's because, they were so busy in reaching the mountain that they put their happiness at stake, and as a result what they got was only the success, a success without peace and happiness is hollow. Therefore, don't rush to be successful, instead, polish yourself the best way possible and learn the art to navigate through your lows and highs. Believe in yourself and with this I wish you an awesome day ahead, and just be you.

Good morning! Embrace this new day with a progressive mindset. Sometimes, the past haunts us to the core and sickens our mindset. The biggest challenge to the new beginnings is to get over with your past. If I recall in my case, for the past 17 years I became a prisoner of my past. My recent trip to Ecuador reminded me of my power to liberate myself from the challenging thoughts that pull me back. The amazon jungle gave me immense courage to let go of the past and look forward, with a wider horizon. I learnt to feel fresh and light, that can only happen when you free yourself from the regrets and the choices that we made in the past. Remember, we had no control back then but now you know how to get a hold of yourself. This is the day of redefining your strength and ability. Cherish your present state, be happy and just be you.

Good morning. For those who truly know me, I've been recognized as both stoic and a workaholic. I am gradually realizing the importance of heeding my own advice. Recognizing that we don't have to figure out our entire life all at once and that there's no need for shame in our current situation, recognizing that and embracing that is crucial. Instead, we can focus on one small thing each day to move closer to our goals, whether it's finding a new job, cultivating a strong and secure relationship, or tidying up our living space. Progressing slowly and steadily, taking one tiny step at a time with patience and perseverance, will ultimately lead us to where we aspire to be. Life is an incredible journey that demands living it to the fullest, striving to become the best versions of ourselves, or at least as much as we can be. Take care, have a great day, and just be yourself.

Good morning! I beg your pardon as today's message is going to be lengthy but I wanted to open up my biggest fear that will somehow help all of you. But I've discovered that I like this new story the new narrative better, and I like who I have become, how I feel every day about me and my future. I know struggle is hard, and talking about your goals is easy but pursuing them is an amazing journey. Don't be shy, don't be afraid and don't ever fear to take the chance. If it truly matters to us, it doesn't matter how long it takes us. What matters is that we get there. I'm very proud of how I've handled the challenges of the last few months. I made a major pivot that reshaped my life in a way that wasn't planned or even predicted. The silent battles that I fought made me humble and strong; the temporary things don't matter to me anymore. All these battles have made me celebrate my strength and the journey I have been through. I leave messages every day to you so that you can celebrate your strength, your power and you can hold onto hope. Have a great day and just be you because you are awesome.

Happy sunshine! Embrace the dawn of a new day, marked by another fresh start filled with hope and self-assurance. The mountain standing before you will eventually be a distant memory, barely visible when you glance back. Yet, the person you evolve into while overcoming that mountain will endure, a testament to your journey of learning and perseverance. The essence of the mountain is to serve as a reminder to savor life's little joys amid its challenges and rewards. In the future, we will look back and realize that these seemingly small moments were, in fact, significant ones. You don't need to be captive to your challenges, past, or fears; we all hold the keys to our own liberation. So, take a breath, reflect, embrace, and cherish each moment. Wishing you a fantastic day; just be yourself.

Good morning! As I look back on my life, the last couple of months. I realize that every time I thought I was being rejected from something good or someone I was getting redirected to something much better for me like goal that I was afraid to chase. Or a dream yet to be realized or set. And as I reflected, after several deaths of family members, and dear friend, I concluded that my spirit, energy, mind, body and soul is my strongest team and once I bring them all together, I can bring out the best from me. I value and respect all my friends so on this day enjoy, remember and breathe. With this message, have a great day and just be you

Rise and shine! Enter this new day filled with opportunities for fresh starts. The key to happiness today lies in allowing each situation to unfold naturally, without imposing preconceived expectations. Regardless of the challenges you may be facing, believe in yourself, honor your worth, understand your value, and stay true to your principles. Always remember your authentic self because if you don't make sacrifices for what you truly desire, your desires might end up being the sacrifice. Persevere, infuse your life with adventures rather than material possessions, and collect stories to share, not just things to display. Step through the door today and radiate your awesomeness, be amazing, be the sunshine that brightens others' days. Bring joy to those you encounter, and above all, have a fantastic day just being yourself.

Good morning! Embarking on a new journey may feel daunting but know that every journey is beautiful with its own set of challenges. With this accept the change and start a fantastic day, filled with fresh insights and new goals. One valuable lesson I've learned this year is the profound distinction between having time and making time. Choose wisely, promise carefully, and commit with conviction. If you find yourself on a path you dislike, remember there's always time to discover another one. Keep some space in your heart for the unimaginable, and, especially during this Christmas season, open your hands to give and your heart to feel. Have a wonderful day, and simply be yourself.

Good Morning! Today's message revolves around happiness and inner peace. In our hectic lives, we often overlook that happiness doesn't solely stem from acquiring something new. Yesterday, I had a realization and came to appreciate that my happiness is rooted in what I already possess, the unconditional love of my kids, my health, and the strength to return to school despite daily doubts about my intelligence and commitment to succeed. My joy manifests at day's end when I celebrate being myself because of the things and people around me that make me feel special. We can't truly appreciate rainbows without understanding doubt, overcoming fears and challenges, or wiping away tears. So accept who you are, pursue that rainbow, let those tears flow, share a hug, and, most importantly, seize the day and just be you.

Good morning! Arriving at a crossroads, faced with life-altering choices, is always an intimidating experience. However, in the past few months, I've come to realize a newfound courage within me. Recognizing that the courage it took to depart from the organization I played a significant role in building and nurturing was an integral part of my identity. I've slowly acknowledged that it no longer resonates with who I actually am. This awareness has empowered me to understand that the same courage that led me to leave will guide me to where I need to be. I noticed a shift in my behavior as the pain of remaining surpassed the fear of change. Consequences and events provided the necessary impetus for me to pursue my newfound peace. So, today, seek our own peace, not someone else's. Find our unique place, not a shared one. Be awesome, be amazing, have a great day, and most importantly, just be you.

Good morning my lovely readers! My message today is about looking ahead, being insightful, being strategic, and, most of all, believing in yourself. Always know that there is a future you haven't seen yet so stay strong and always look forward to brighter days. Just because you're smarter than others, does not mean you will belittle the people around you. I have learned that patience is both silent and powerful, it will continue to bring unexpected meaning to our lives, to our existence and purpose in these times of celebration. Respect your body and your mind when they are asking you to take a break and honor yourself when you need a moment for yourself. When I look back at my life, I see pain, mistakes, and heartache, but that is not our narrative because when we look in the mirror, we see our strength. Learned lessons give us a reason to be proud of overcoming a challenge or barrier that shaped us into who we are. We are awesome, and we are amazing. Have a great day, and just be you.

Good morning! Today, we should believe and trust the divine process because you never know what the next moment will have for us. It could be life-changing. Never underestimate the power of what the next moment has in store for us. Always trust that no matter how big the storm is, you will always be stronger. Remember that life's journey is full of surprises, challenges, and amazing moments. Today could be the day when you'll receive your miracle or the gift that you've been waiting for. When the stars shine on you, the sun brightens its gifts on you, so never stop trusting, cherishing, and always have room for something amazing to appear. Have an awesome day, and just be you.

Good morning to all the amazing people! Today's message will revolve around our day. The present day, no matter how hard the past day had been, but today you have to enjoy your first breath and embrace what lies ahead of you. Today, you need to muster the strength, know that you're strong enough to climb any mountain challenge, any obstacle, and defy the odds. The more you focus on what you want in life, the quicker it becomes your reality. Living life with confidence is sometimes misunderstood as arrogance, but it's actually the realization that you don't have to compare yourself to anyone. Focus on being the best version of yourself. Be proud of your accomplishments. Be proud of overcoming many challenges because life is a journey full of hills, mountains, and obstacles. Only you know how to get through them for you, so have a great day, and just be you.

Good morning! Today, I will shout out to all my friends for the success they have achieved so far. Each day does not bring huge success. Huge success comes once in a lifetime. But, you need to realize that every day is a new success, yesterday, when you found it tough to come out of bed due to low strength, and today, when you showed the best in you at your workplace. These small things are making way for your big success. Just because you never let anyone see your tough moments, it doesn't mean that you didn't face any challenges. Every step you are taking in the direction you have set for yourself is indicating the new you. We all should take the chance to choose and change our lives for the better. Do what makes us smile, dance, laugh, and rejoice. With this, have an amazing day and just be you.

Good morning, my friends, and awesome people! Today's message may sound bitter, but it's a lesson to inspire us to make us believe in ourselves. Some people may never support you because they are afraid of what you might become. I may not be the best at what I do, but I know I never cheated on someone, and this feeling brings me contentment and peace. Human beings are designed to remember bad times more than good times because when we struggle, we cry for a week, and when we succeed, we celebrate for a day. Isn't it cruel? We must appreciate our victories and successes a little more than we normally do. I've seen more dark days that I want to remember, and these dark days made me strong, or maybe I was already strong, and these moments made me prove it. If there's anything that these last couple of years taught me, especially the last couple of months, it is that life changes with no warning, no matter how prepared you seem to be, so there is no reason to continue to look back on it. When we have so much to look forward to being awesome, be great. Have a great day, and just be you.

Good morning. The past few days have been personally overwhelming, prompting me to remind myself to be the reason people believe in the goodness of the world. I recognize that you and I are two amazing individuals who never fail. Yes, you read it right; we don't fail until we accept failure. As I reflect, I've decided that 2024 will mark a transformative year for me. Mentally, physically, and most importantly, spiritually, though not in a conventional church or ceremony manner. I'm defining this personally, acknowledging my higher power. Committing to the continuous improvement of myself, I'm embracing the belief that I can achieve all that I set my mind to. Acknowledging our flaws and addressing negative behaviors is essential for self-change. Witnessing the sunlight and positive energy entering someone's heart after they've been in a dark place for an extended period is one of the most beautiful things in the world. In 2023, I chose my awakening, a new beginning, understanding that without rain, nothing grows. So, today, set goals, be genuine, be honest with yourself, and just believe because you are amazing. You are awesome. Have a great day, and, most importantly, just be you.

Good morning, my friend. You are an integral part of my circle, and I understand that there are days when fatigue and stress take a toll. I want you to know that together we have your back. Sending these positive morning messages, or as some see them, daily blessings is my way of consistently reminding you that I'm always here, supporting you. You hold the paintbrush to your daily outcomes, and your days are only as grey as you allow them to be. Find a reason to laugh or smile each day; it might not add years to your life, but it will undoubtedly add life to your years. Today, consider making it the first day you change the way you think, and you'll observe how your life transforms alongside it. Your thoughts will serve as guides for your daily energy, spirit, and hope. I've personally learned and chosen not to lead a positive life if I'm consistently thinking negatively. These messages serve as a reminder that, just as I have people in my corner, I'm here for you in your corner. Keep moving forward, and don't fret about your speed; progress is progress, regardless of its pace. Dream, laugh, smile, hope these are your pillars. Have a great day, and, most importantly, just be you.

Good morning! Today, I pondered over a message for a while because it's the end of the year but also a new beginning to the next year. Let's reflect on some of the best things in life. They need not be grand. Even the small things can be big depending on how you give importance to them. We take our small achievements for granted and forget that big success could not have been possible due to this small milestone. This past year, we won, we cried, we laughed, but most of all, we learned from those moments, and they left us with a lesson to take forward. Always remember that our greatest treasure is our family and those friends who are part of our extended family. We may not be perfect, and we may have a few nuts in our families, but we love them with all our hearts, so we end this year with the idea of believing that something amazing is about to happen. Focus on the positive, embrace your will to believe, and trust yourself. Have a great day, and just be you.

Greetings, my dear friends! Today marks the commencement of a splendid year, a fresh start filled with promise. I'm here to impart a profound message to each one of you. Keep in mind that the fundamental essence of life lies in embracing peace and happiness. As we navigate the journey of life and maturity, contemplation about altering our paths puzzles us. I've personally experienced this, as have many of you. However, without acting, these thoughts remain mere thoughts. Each day presents an opportunity to decide, and I encourage you to make today that pivotal day that becomes a turning point in your life. Take every day as an opportunity and embrace the richness of the moment. Be grateful for what you have today and strive to acquire better in life, have great day and just be you.

Good morning! Hello, my friends, on this second day of a new beginning. I want to share today's reflection with you. Maintaining a positive outlook every day and sharing these thoughts doesn't imply that I'm happy all the time. Instead, it signifies that even on challenging days, I hold onto the belief that better days lie ahead; with this belief, let's continue to a journey with faith, belief, and positivity. My daily messages aim to provide you with three essential things: the confidence to recognize your self-worth, the strength to pursue your dreams, and the understanding of how deeply you are loved and cherished. Through my own struggles, I've learned an important lesson, appreciating what we have before life teaches you to value what we've lost. With this be happy and embrace the things and people around you, and remember just be you.

Good morning today! Life is full of surprises. I've learned to become content with the choices I've made. There are times in life when we take decisions without contemplating the consequences. But the aftermath of those decision is not pleasing in life. And our guilt makes it even tougher. People punish themselves more, and it worsens the situation. The wise ones are those who accept their decisions and work to rectify their mistakes. It's time to prioritize yourself once again because how you treat yourself establishes the standard for how others should treat you. Refuse to settle for anything less than respect. Lastly, live your life not for the sake of being noticed but for your absence to leave an impact. You are awesome and have a presence that is indispensable in both our personal and professional world. Just be you.

Good morning! Have you ever pondered over what the first thing to do when you wake up is? The first thing you do when you wake up is to be grateful for yet another day to conquer. The foremost blessing is our sound health and our ability to survive in the competitive world. We need to love ourselves and pave the path of positive energy. Every challenge we face on the journey of life doesn't work the way we want it to this is not the way of life. A decent approach to life is accepting its adversities and using it to enhance yourself as much as you can. You don't want to end, but you will have to keep going to succeed and make an impact in your life. Certain stories give us great hindsight of how things can go wrong; such stories reshape our notions and reveal the true essence of life, and that is to stand firmly and steadfastly in your life. Have a great day and just be you.

Happy sunshine, my friends! This day, we vow to enjoy ourselves and live in our present. On this day, we will display our true selves without any fear of judgment and failure. Today, we aim to get rid of all the norms that have kept us restricted and hurdles our growth and prosperity. This message is just for you and I. You may decide to enjoy your day in whatever way suits you, either by making your favorite meal, hanging out with friends, or dancing to your favorite song and then laughing until it doesn't scare you anymore. If you want to have a better tomorrow, let's start working on a better version of us today. I have realized that soul friends recognize each other by the vibes they radiate through their strong appearance and kind attitude. Sometimes, it requires the worst pain to bring out the best version of us, so set the target, chase the goal, and remember you are the best. Have a great day, and just be you.

Good morning! As I start the day, my initial reflection is directed towards the past: "Dear past, thank you for the memories and lessons." Looking ahead, I am prepared and eager for what the future holds. With that in mind, I encourage you to embrace the best version of yourself. Since my teenage years, I have made a pivotal decision, and I want to share that choice with you. Don't allow anyone to dismiss your dreams as too grand or claim you cannot bring your ambitious aspirations to fruition. Let your journey be fueled by hope, faith, the support of friends, unwavering drive, and the determination to succeed. Your greatness is within you. Wishing you a fantastic day, and remember, just be you.

Greetings, brilliant friends! I hope you slept well last night and are ready to embrace the day ahead. I made a choice earlier this year. If we don't make the time to create a life that we want, we will most probably be living a monotonous and gloomy life. Life is the name of exploration, hardship, and trial, and it's the beauty of life that brings new challenges that allow us to look outside the box. I have learned to make sure that the big difference in our daily process is to always to wake up and stay positive. Your mornings should be filled with a positive outlook towards life. Do it for three weeks and notice a significant change in your mood and life. Embrace today and just be you.

On February 1, 2022, I chose to love myself more and trust myself more because that is who I will be spending the rest of my life with and so will my life partner. The one we choose to be our life partner deserves to be happy and content with us. That requires self-love and acceptance towards the life we live. We need to be happy and confront the issues that are stressful. To sort out this issue, I started to do a daily journal, which became these morning messages, which I share with my friends daily. They help me as much as they help the people, I share them with. The goal is to build someone up and put their insecurities of choice behind them. Remind them every day that we are worthy. And in some form, I try to tell them they're magical. To be the shining light in a dim moment too often, cherish your spirit, and replenish your soul with good energy and positive thoughts. Have a great day, and just be you.

Good morning! Congratulations, you made it to another day. Today, we will celebrate a new beginning and a new threshold. Every day, I learn that the challenge of starting over the hardest things is to let go of the trauma and the drama of your former self. But I've also known that every time I subtract negativity, I make more room for the positive, so I breathe, and something meaningful comes my way. With this message, just smile and have a great day. Remember to be happy and just be you.

Good morning! I have a simple message for you today. Don't look back with regret. Look forward with hope. Don't waste your energy worrying over things that are not in your control. Use your energy to believe and prioritize peace. Peace might feel comfortable to many, but in actuality, it's not comfort; it's more about working hard without any fear of judgment. Just be yourself and continue the path of success and accomplishment. The moment you keep aside all the worries, you realize that the opportunities have started to unfold, and it's all due to your passion for acceptance. Whatever triggers you should be abandoned and breathe in positive air. Now smile with your peace of spirit and energy. Have a great day, and just be you.

Good morning! Today, I will share two important thoughts with you all. As I reflect on my past, I realize that my past has made me strong as a single parent. I learned many lessons, but the most profound one of them is about the struggles that we face in today's world. On the other hand, I realized that my children are not a distraction for me and my important work. In fact, they are the most important figures in my life. They bring me joy, contentment, and hope. This is due to them that I am motivated to live a fulfilling life. The second lesson is about getting new directions in your life. There comes a time in life when you walk away from all the drama, and those people who create it and make us miserable are usually the ones who are most near us. This is why you should always be very vigilant while choosing your friends. This way, you will be safe from numerous things. With this, all I have for you is to have a great day and just be you.

Rise and shine! Today's message is very simple; it's about embracing the new day, new thoughts of positive energy, and discovering the new you. Many people get mistaken in recognizing who they really are. We claim to like and dislike certain things, but we don't really know what we really want, and then there is a point where you realize that the thing you liked the most isn't that valuable. This is the point in life when we know that even we as humans deceive ourselves in many ways, whether knowingly or unknowingly. We never put ourselves deliberately on trial; if we do, it can help us recognize where we belong. With this amazing day, I will suggest you all try new things that can reveal your true self, embrace this new day and just be you.

Good morning! I know it's not simple to perceive the phenomenon of life every time. Having been aware that life is another name for hardships, we, being human, become disconcerted over the matters that surpass our control. Sometimes things are complicated, but time and space help us figure everything out; all it requires is true belief and perseverance. My advice to you would be not to rush into anything, to feel the moment, and to give yourself time because the only way to be happy with our choices is to realize our thoughts, emotions, actions, and decisions that are directly proportional to our well-being. Our life is our responsibility, and we must make the most of it by having a positive outlook toward it and just be you.

Good morning! Life is tough and throws us challenges that we don't think we deserve. Sometimes, we are so vulnerable that we lack the power to fight but remember that strength only comes after you have undergone a trial. That phase of our lives reveals our true strength. When our hearts are broken, we find a way to keep moving forward. No matter what life throws at us, we must remind ourselves of our strength to move forward. As I get older, I have learned it's okay to live a life that no one else understands, so have a great day and just be you.

Good day, my friends! I realize you can't always have good days, but the goal is to face those bad days with a great attitude. You may not always see the results of your kindness, but with every bit of positive energy we contribute to the people around us, we strive to make the world a better place for the upcoming generations. With this message, have a great day, and just be you.

Morning greetings! Don't be afraid to take that first step today. It is a gateway to your success because you don't know what is kept for you. So, don't lose any opportunity and accept the challenges that feel daunting, but you never know what is saved for you. One profound thing to remember is to trust your instincts. Your instinct is a clear message from the people before you, it's going to be the beginning of many great things. Be grateful for all the things you have in your life, and you will see a lot more beauty in your world. Have a great day, and just be you.

Good morning! Let's start our morning with four great things that matter in life's journey that I want to share with you all.

1. Take care of your thoughts when you are alone and take care of your words when people surround you.

2. Always end your days with a positive thought, no matter how things end.

3. Tomorrow is a fresh opportunity to make it better. So, never drain your energy into regretting what has gone.

4. Finally, random hug matters because you never know how much people need it in this fast-paced world. At the right time by the right person, like a child, it will take all your stress and worry away.

So have a great day and just be you.

Good morning! Start your day with the thought that you reflect your ideas. Think positive, act positive. We must teach our hearts to accept the failures and move forward. Never stop learning because life never stops teaching, and always remember that kindness does not cost a thing, but this is the richest gift we can give at the right moment. Finally, don't overthink your challenges. Choose well, do what makes you happy, have a kind heart, and just be you.

Good morning. Smile a lot today. It makes us more attractive and appealing. Smiles change our moods and the moods of people around us; they relieve stress and help us stay positive. We need to understand that we cannot skip steps in the process of being happy. If we try to cut an action, we end up just getting hurt. Let's take a lesson from the butterflies and give ourselves time to grow, heal, and transform. Only then will we be able to soar high. So have a great day, and until tomorrow , just be you.

Good morning, my people! Today's reminder is a profound message; it's about counting on the marvelous for our own affairs. When we wake up every morning, we should remember how beautiful our journey can be with the choices we make. Our choices are what transform us as a person. We need to realize the importance of the decisions we make for our future; they are the ones that rule over our emotions. Our life is based on the choices we make, so be wise when opting for anything or any person. Listen to your intuition and follow your gut feeling. With this, I wish you an incredible day and just be you.

Good morning! Today, I have a very simple message for you. Don't use your energy to worry about the future. The future is something that you have no control over; you can only control your present by being productive and making efforts. Instead of wasting your energy over something uncontrollable, use it to believe, work hard, grow, and succeed. Establish trust, grow, and heal; no one is sent by accident to this world. We need to be thankful for who and what we have in our lives because we will end up having more than we ever imagined. Listen, see, and breathe. Have an amazing day, and just be you.

Good morning! I learned an important lesson on this trip to Phoenix, all of my plans did not come together; they didn't work out the way I had thought they would, and this is how life rules us all. I have learned that regretting over the past things is not wise. The smart ones live in the present; they make efforts and utilize their energy for the right thing. Never feel you're a burden or that you are not making it right; always remember that you're here for a reason. We might not be smart enough to contemplate it right, but a higher power has sent us all with something tremendous to look forward to. Never let down the faith that a higher power had in you. With this message, take the decision that aligns with your soul and work for betterment; those who strive for betterment never go astray. Have an amazing day, and just be you.

Happy sunny day! Remember to value the effort of a person who tries to keep in touch with you. It's not everyone who tries to stay in touch. It shows their level of care and sincerity for you. Their way of talking represents their feelings for you. These are the ones who choose to remain your friends, and they are the real gems to hold onto. If you have been ignoring your loved ones for quite some time, then today is the day when you can make them feel important. Gestures of love never get ignored, be it small. To loved ones, everything counts, be it a few-minute conversation. Just be you.

Good morning! Today, I have a deep message for you. Believe that someday, all the love you've given away will find its way back to you and finally stay with you. Stay kind and sincere to the people, and never let any harsh comment make you feel down. Don't pay attention to the mean comments; instead, take it as a growth opportunity and strive harder to succeed. Believe me, when you hit the peak of success, you don't have to worry about someone's opinion of you. Just continue the journey of exploration and become the best version of yourself. Love, respect, grow with all your might, and exhibit the best in you. Just be you.

Good morning! There is no greater wealth in this world than peace of mind and no greater gift than the support and love of a dear friend. The unconditional love of the people around us excites us to make progress in life. If you have a bad mood and mindset, brighten it up by wearing a wide smile and cherish the positivity around you. Spread happiness and raise awareness about a positive mindset. Your spirit cleanses your soul and fills it with emotions, the emotions that derive from us. So, let's embrace the moments of surprise and happiness. Have a great day, and just be you.

Good morning! A few months ago, when I looked back on my life, I was forced to see pain, mistakes, and heartache, and then I chose to reflect on it when I looked in the mirror today. I see my strength, I see the scars from lessons learned, but most importantly, I know pride in myself because I chose new options, and if you can see it, you can achieve it. Even though your journey is long and strenuous, remember that every step forward is a moment of success and achievement. Focus on the positive and let the negativity fade away; your positive spirit should be strong enough to lead you toward the path of success. Just be you.

Good morning!! Yesterday was a nice day for me when I got the ultimate compliment from someone. I work with an advisory Council; they complimented me on how I always stand by my values and my ethics, even if most people don't understand. I take pride in being referred to as the most disciplined individual. So, my message today is that let's learn to be gentle with our souls to trust our values even when the world is harsh around us. Go easy on yourself when the struggles have been difficult and challenging; take the time to feel what is required in that moment. It is during these moments that we understand ourselves the most. We learn to love ourselves more completely. And that kind of love will carry us through to brighter days.

Good morning! Today, let's celebrate to be grateful for every second of every day. I love life, and that's the most precious gift that has been given to us by our mothers. Life is very precious, and we need to accept both compliments and criticism because it takes sun and rain to grow a flower. Allowing people in your life is a beautiful thing and letting go of people who drain your spirit is another beautiful thing you can do to make your life worth it. The key to being happy is recognizing your power and choosing what to accept and what to let go. I choose happiness and you should also prioritize your sanity. Have a great day, and just be you.

Good morning! Today, we will talk about relationships and friendships that play a crucial role in shaping our mindset. The situation isn't always ideal; great friendships, and relationships aren't great because they have no problems, they are great because of the people involved, their sacrifices and, most importantly, their understanding of each other. To make the relationships work out, it's important to have an unbiased opinion and see the thing openly. Relationships tend to grow and evolve as it is the part of the journey. The world is not a place to remain stagnant, in fact, it's a sign of weakness or a lack of faith. On the contrary, the price of caring and loving relationship is to see things beyond norms and put sincere effort to build a healthy and everlasting bond, guided by the idea of just be you.

Good morning! Reflecting on the conversation that I had with one of my mentors when he asked me when the last time I reviewed or looked at my personal strategic plan, I replied with a smile and said it's been a while and he reminded me of the old saying "Dream written down with date becomes a goal, a goal broken down into steps, becomes a plan and finally a planned backed by actions makes your dreams come true." It created an everlasting impact on my mind, and I believe as we evolve and grow, pivot, and work towards achieving our purpose, our path guides us to the happy place, and you choose to have a great day. Just be you!

Good afternoon! Today, I have a message for you. Remember that you are loved and cherished by your family and your friends, you are important, and you matter. We sometimes forget who we are because we feel like we have been lost or forgotten for so long because of our careers, education, or parenting. We forget what it was like to be ourselves, to be carefree and independent. So, today, embrace the lessons, embrace the love, embrace all the discoveries of who you are, and remember just to be you.

Good morning! A profound realization that I came across some days ago is that mistakes are painful, but as time goes by, they become a collection of experiences called lessons. Your knowledge and your experience are your greatest asset, and every time you share it, it brings more value to your life and your personality, so remember, nothing is impossible. Everything is possible, and if you step back, the word means I'm possible. Have a great day, and just be you.

Good day! Here comes a new day with a new message. Start your day with a refreshing mindset and a broader horizon toward life and its complexities. Today, let's choose to forgive ourselves for what we perceive as our past mistakes. Today, let's choose happiness, contentment, and inner peace. Today, let us free ourselves of negativity and take ownership of our lives. Today and every day moving forward, let's choose self-love and believe in the magic of undying hope. There is so much beauty in the world that is yet to be discovered, and the most beautiful creature of on earth is all that is living and thriving. So, moving forward, let's not give up on ourselves no matter what is going on in our life. We might be facing battles that the world is unaware of, but let's believe in our worth, understand our value, embrace our truth, and bring joy to life. Have a great day, and just be you.

Good morning! Today's reminder is to never stop living, never stop laughing, and never stop loving. Don't forget about the inner value of hope; remember and gather your strength in the things that give you inner peace, satisfaction, and happiness. Have an awesome day and just be you.

Good morning! A few months ago, I realized I had a superpower, and that is hope. It was one of the greatest realizations and happiest moments of my life; it was that morning when I found the courage to let go of the things that were beyond my control. That morning, I contemplated the power of forgiving yourself and moving on with life. I cannot change my ah-ha moment, but I have the courage and strength to not be afraid to start all over again. To give things a fresh start, as my failure was not the end of my life. The message that I must share with you today is never to lose hope or be sad. One day, you will thank yourself for not giving up the struggles back then and developing the strength we need for tomorrow. So today, don't think so much; just do what makes you happy and just be you.

Good morning! So today I am sharing life's lessons with you. And that is to understand what our higher power is trying to reveal upon us. Sometimes, we become so busy in life that we don't see the signals. In this world or this rat race, when some calamities appear, we need to calm ourselves down and contemplate the need of that situation. It's indeed very true that our emotions take a toll on us and leave us shattered, but is it all? Should we not rise and leave the past behind? Should we not link it with our greater plan. Yes, we should! There are always two ways in life: one is to sit back and mourn what's left behind, and the other is to use that chance to overpower your intelligence. Yes! You read it right; the best way to use your intelligence is in the darkest of moments. Because this is the time when our brain thinks impossible. So, use your gloomy moments to empower yourself and live wisely. Have a great day, and just be you.

Good morning to all my people! I learned on my trip to Ecuador last year that a rough patch of road can lead to a beautiful spiritual place. So, believe with full might that the best is yet to come. Let's make today the day we choose because if we don't leave our past in the past, it will destroy the path of our future. Live for what today has to offer, not for what yesterday has taken away. I share my past with you not to make you feel sorry for me but so to impart to you the thought that I am driven through my experiences. If you feel pain, you're still living life. To stumble is a human act, and as long as you keep trying, there is still hope, and I share my messages because I don't underestimate the power of planting seeds so have a great day and just be you.

Rise and shine! A small reminder for today. As we view the morning sun for the first time today, don't forget that waking up each day should be the first thing we should be grateful for. Sometimes we just must appreciate where we are. We have come a long way, and we are still learning and growing so today let's be proud of ourselves. Life becomes more beautiful when it is filled with compassion, accomplishment, reflection, happiness, and joy. With this have a great day and just be you

Good morning! Living a life of service to your community and being genuine in your interactions can create meaningful connections and contribute positively to the world around you. It's also commendable that you've chosen not to apologize when it's not warranted, as this reflects a commitment to honesty and self-respect. Remember that life is indeed a continuous journey of learning and growth. Embracing your uniqueness, dancing to the rhythm of your own life, and having faith in your decisions can lead to a more genuine and fulfilling experience. Live happy and just be you!

Good morning! The most rewarding feeling you can feel is the acknowledgment that you took a step in the right direction. You took a step towards the future where everything that you never thought possibly became possible in that realization. Sometimes, having coffee with your best friend is all the therapy you need, and it's not what we have in our lives that makes us happy, but it's who we have in our lives that matters the most. So be thankful for all your new realizations; positive choice means positive change. Have a great day and just be you.

Good morning! Today, I celebrate my journey, my choices, and my happiness. Life is too short to wake up every day with regret, so I chose to love the people around me and build an eternal connection with them. I chose the people who treated me right and left those behind who were resentful of my success. I believe everything happens for a reason, and that reason is undeniably the one that shapes our journey. I have vowed to wake up with a new outlook on life. So, today, embrace you and your accomplishments, big or small; they are part of your journey. Have a great day, wear a wide smile, and conquer the world. Just be you.

Good morning! Today we will look beyond the norms. We have always been told by society, school, and our parents to have a plan. To them, it's very important to follow your goal, and that can only happen when you have a full-fledged plan. What we don't realize is that every moment of your life cannot be planned. You cannot plan every moment of your life; sometimes, leaving things as they are is the smartest step. Not every time do you leave them as is, but there are moments in life when things are beyond our understanding. In those moments, trust the process and don't try to control the situation. Embrace that moment, that day and just be you.

Good morning, my friends! Remember to be happy and cherish your moment with the little that we have. There are people with fewer things, but they still manage to smile. So, today, live with happiness and joy not because everything is good but because you can see the good side of everything. Your gratitude makes sense of your past; it brings you peace for today and then creates your vision for the future. Take the first step and choose to shine. Have a great day, and just be you.

Good morning! As I was walking through the streets of Vancouver yesterday, I thought we had been worrying about our whole life preparing for the future. The very moment I realized my future is not about getting successful, but it's more about being satisfied with where we are in our lives. We are so naïve to comprehend that our happiness is linked with us only. We are the ones who should embrace change and go with the flow. It's so ironic that we depend on others for everything, be it our own happiness, but we fail to realize that other people are not responsible for us. All these thoughts overwhelmed me, and I decided never to rely on anyone for my happiness. I just had an awesome visit. I cried in my car because I was happy. With this, have an awesome day, and just be yourself.

Good morning! Today, we will talk about reflection. Sometimes, this word sounds weird, but it has a profound meaning. When you reflect on who you really are, you conclude your real self. We should all take some time to look inside of us and reflect on ourselves. After taking my Friday evening walk in Vancouver, I was driving back home when I realized two very important things. The first is a smile, and second is a kind gesture. These two things mean 1000 great things in a positive way to someone who needs them, but they can also hide 1000 problems or challenges faced by people. This phenomenon reminded me that I have too many flaws to ever think I was perfect, lol. I have way too many blessings to be grateful for, so let's be real and lay a strong foundation of happiness and satisfaction. Unhappiness is never the situation; it's our thoughts of unhappiness. Embrace your gifts, see through the fog, find your joy, be happy, smile, breathe, and be grateful. In the end, I would say just be you.

Good morning! Time and good friends are the precious things that I highly value. We cannot heal the past by dwelling there. Instead, we heal the past by fully embracing and living in the present. Let go of your tears and live your life to the fullest. Fear is not a sign of weakness; it takes courage and emotional strength to release the inner pain of your past, so continue to be courageous, strong, full of happiness and joyous guided by hope. With this message, I wish you an awesome day and just be you.

Good morning! Let's look around at the role models we look up to and who play a crucial role in our lives. Remember that our own personal heroes are the very source for us to soar high. Ensure that we are in control of our mind in our world, our inner peace. Let's pay attention to what we think, what we believe in, and how we process our emotions. As we notice, there's not enough room in our minds or spirits for worry and hope, so we must decide which gets to live in our mind and spirit, hope tells us there's no shortcut to happiness. We must take every step to rise above pain, sorrow, and worry and rely on the perseverance of hope, so live today with a smile and laughter and just be yourself.

Good morning!! Some days are so hard on us that we cannot even function for simple tasks. In those days, we need to remember our true strength; we need to understand that it's also a phase of our lives and this too shall pass. Never let the days with weak energy weaken you; always believe in the best outcomes, and that is only possible with the best input, remember the best input is perseverance and self-belief, no matter what pace you follow. Always be mindful of nature's phenomenon that if you're moving, you will reach somewhere. It might take some time, but the result is guaranteed. Have a day of great moments and just be you.

Good morning! Every day, we wake up with a challenge; it doesn't matter whether we are ready for that challenge or not. Bit by bit, as we put our trust in ourselves and work hard with a strong belief, things start falling into place. There are always two options modes, whether to accept the challenge or reject the challenge. The one who accepts the challenge is a keen learner who does not fear change. On the contrary, the one who rejects the challenge is happy with what they have. Those that do not strive for better, does not set an example in society. I read somewhere that if you're born poor, it was not your fault but if you die poor, it certainly is your fault. Therefore, spend your life wisely and make an impact in society. Just be you.

Good morning!! Today I want to share my summary thinking of the week when life gives you 1000 reasons to break down and cry or just say I'm done. These feelings are real, and we have been there sometime in our lives. In that moment of self-doubt, pause, take a deep breath, and follow a path of happiness and satisfaction and just be you.

Good morning! Today is the day of taking pride in who we are and how far we have come. So, let's be proud of ourselves and embrace the accomplishments we have made by pushing ourselves to become the best versions of ourselves. With this, I wish you an awesome day and just be you.

Rise and Shine! Today, be the reason for someone's smile, today, treat someone just as you wanted to be treated, today, spread happiness and be the reason for someone's belief in goodness. With this, take care of yourself and your loved ones and be happy. Just be you.

Good morning! I start my morning by being grateful to my higher power for the blessings that have been sent my way. I prefer to rise early in the morning so that I have enough time to ponder over the blessings I have and be grateful to my higher power for the immeasurable love for me. I am sure many of you are also so blessed in so many ways; all we need to have been the sense of realization. So today, be grateful for what you have and live your life to the fullest. Know that you are deeply valued and respected by your people have a great day and just be you.

Good morning! I'd often annoy people with my overwhelming thoughts. I then realized that the people I share my feelings with are not worth it. As I have evolved as a person, I often reflect or respond harshly on current situations. I don't sit back and cry over the things that are beyond my control. Instead, I figure out a way to contemplate and work in the best way possible as per my capacity. When things are uncontrollable, I leave them and decide to be happy with what I have. My suggestion to you all is, don't stress about the things that you cannot work out. Leave them and be ready to receive even more of what you sent out into the world. Just be you.

Good morning! Happiness is a choice, and those who value it try to acquire it. I have seen many people underestimate the real power of this emotion. We don't realize that being happy is not only an emotion; it's a process of transformation. It's a process when you realize the power of your hormones that can enable you to soar high and make the impossible possible. Joy and happiness are a choice. I am happy and excited about my life right now. I have my moments. Always remember that the good outweighs the bad, no matter what. With this, I would recommend you all choose happiness and just be you.

Good morning! I remind myself today that we need to throw away the idea that haunts us. We need to live lives free of fear and dependency. We need to be kind to ourselves; we should let go of our not-so-wise decisions. We need to realize that humans err, and it's normal. The more we put pressure on ourselves, the more unproductive we become. Therefore, live happily and let go of the things that bother you. Be brave and just be you.

Good morning, my people! In our daily lives, we face many challenges that hinder our growth, but do they really hinder it, or do we just perceive it as a hindrance? The things that seem to be obstacles are not really obstacles; in fact, they shape us for resilience and strength. Therefore, embracing the new challenges and in our day-to-day challenges, our self-worth is our one of our most challenging insecurities for the most part. Self-worth is an understanding at the intellectual level, grounded on the idea that trusting it is, it to heart level and accepting it is at our soul level, is that we are worthy. Believe your worthiness, it is proven by our very existence, by every breath we take to survive and the beating of our heart that is the collection of the biorhythms of the generations before us. Recognize your ability and self-worth. You are someone's 7th generation, and your role is vital for the next 7 generations, so cherish it because you're the one to bring change. Have a great day, and just be you.

Good morning! With this peaceful morning, I would like to tell you that a peaceful life is all that matters. In this chaotic world, be someone who leaves a positive impact, be the reason for someone's brightness. For this, you need to have a good heart and be considerate of what you bring to the table. Have a great day, and just be you.

Good morning! I often ponder the fact that getting up every morning is nothing but an utter privilege. We're so occupied with complaining about our miserable lives that we even forget to be grateful to for what we have been given, another day. So be and just be you.

Good morning! Today, we vow to embrace our days with positive energy and the new memories ahead. I have realized that sometimes we miss the most beautiful things in our lives without realizing their worth. So, open your mind, your eyes, and your spirit, and you will see that the thought to that message is that you close the door to your past and open the door to your future. Take a deep breath, rub your eyes, wear a wide smile, and start the next chapter of your life. Have a great day, and just be you.

Good morning! Every moment is fraught with love, and every hour is fraught with happiness. It is just our perception that does not let us live in peace. Every time you lose something, do not blame yourself; instead, contemplate yourself, analyze that mistake, and restart to experience new mistakes. Yes, you read it right. Your life is the name of experience, and experience is a set of emotions, mistakes, achievements, growth, and what not. So, when you have realized your mistake, move forward, and make a new mistake, as mistakes, along with them, bring lots of powerful lessons and a wider horizon toward life. If we lose that insight, it becomes a faded memory but if you live it, it becomes a happy glorious life so good morning, lol. Do not wait for things to get easier or simpler. Life will always be complicated. Every day, since I changed my outlook on life, I have decided to be happy. Right now, and every day moving forward otherwise we will run out of time, that decision guided my soul and my spirit to recognize that healing does not mean the hurt and pain of previous choices never existed. It means that the hurt and pain no longer controls my life. Have a wonderful day, and just be you.

Good morning!! My friends, I am so happy today that you have made it this far; I have full confidence in you and that you will succeed remarkably in your life. Remember that the creator always gives us two ways to live. One is to live as we are born, and the other is to lead a good and happy life that is full of joy, hope, happiness, and dreams. If we live in a safe way with humble forgiveness and an enlightened spirit, we don't live for ourselves, but we also benefit others and provide them with a path to follow. Your whole life is worth it if you even created an impact on one person, so never back off from doing any good. With this, be happy and just be yourself. We live not just for us but in respect and honor of the seventh generations before us but also for the seven generations from now honor their journey, respect their footsteps, have a great day and go be you.

Good morning my friends! Today I will share with you someone's wise words that brought light to my life. It is a powerful message that will change your perspective towards life. So that great message is about how you can change your life in a minute. And that is to remain calm and wise, in the moments of heat, never react instantly. Instead, be wise and calm and contemplate over the situation. Because calmer minds think wisely and the calmer you become, the more wisdom you will show. Therefore, choose wisely, choose carefully, choose with a good heart, and choose for you. Have a momentous day and just be you.

Good morning!! It is almost a year since I decided to embrace change. A change that I much needed to escape from the same monotonous life. So, I decided to incorporate minor changes in my lifestyle choices. Honestly, I must admit, it was a wonderful experience. It was a great ride that started my day with positive energy, I prioritized peace and hard work and chose to remain busy. Though, it was tough as hell, some days were filled with great motivation whereas some days were a challenge. But I never gave up and continued my journey to the path free of worldly worries. I chose my own happiness, and I did not depend on anyone for my emotional needs. A year ago, I decided to start making changes in the way I look at life and my daily outlook. It has been a great ride starting the day with positive energy and if I wanted inner peace I had to stop complaining about others and I needed to change my outlook and myself. It has been a challenge because sometimes I wake up a warrior, and some days, I wake up a broken mess. There are many days where I am both and these morning messages help me overcome the challenges ahead with a positive outlook. I stopped looking at things as obstacles, but I am more interested in challenges that can be overcome with smart, insightful solutions and positive energy. So, every day I choose to stand, fight, and try. I am the only person trying to be better than the defeated person I used to be, so today, be happy, be positive, enjoy the gift of today, breathe, and just be you.

Good morning! Today, I will share with you all the suffering of my last night. It was a rough night filled with low emotions and weaknesses. I felt low on my emotional strength. My message today is more of a thought or a lesson: imagine if we spread love as quickly as we spread regret, doubt, hate, and negativity; the world would become the most amazing place to live in. With this, let us decide to live happily and spread positivity around us. Be optimistic and just be you.

Good morning, my lovely readers!! This morning should bring liveliness to your life. I understand that moments in our lives are so tough and unneglectable that we cannot let them go off our lives this easily. When you perceive life as difficult, please understand the fact that it is not easier for anyone. Everyone deals with their share of problems; I can tell you the steps to remain calm and composed. When life hits you harder in the face, remember that everything in your life happens for a reason. You might fail to connect the dots at that very time, but with each passing day, things will make sense to you. Enjoy life as an experience, believe that an enjoyable time is coming, have a great day, and just be you.

Happy sunshine, my amazing readers! When we get up early in the morning, we don't realize the importance of a new sun and a new moment. Never underestimate your days; you never know what your higher power has planned for you in the next moment. A new day can be a turning point in your life; you can land a new job, you can learn something new, you can meet new friends, you can meet with the love of your life. So, every new moment brings a new chapter of life. Therefore, never underestimate the power of new chapters in life. One day it just clicked for me. I realized what was enormously important to me and my values and what wasn't. I decided to care less about what people thought or said about me, and I thought more about what I thought of myself. I realized how far I have come, and I remembered all those days and nights when I thought my life was such a mess and how I could not see how I could possibly recover or push past it. Then I took a deep breath, smiled, and reminded myself that we have a roof over our head's food in the cupboard, and I would smile. I was so proud of myself because I fought hard to become the person I am today. Have a great day, and just be you.

Good morning!! Today I will tell you about the strength of our character. We often undervalue the power of our aura. The positive aura tends to spread positivity and happiness around. It radiates the very power of our strength and spread positivity. Sometimes, we want to treat people the way they treat us, but we cannot because that's not our trait. If you react with the same intensity as someone else behaved with you, it will only spread hatred and bitterness in people. Rather, react with positivity and a smile; believe me, you will notice people's changed behavior. You will realize the joy of happiness, and their pain will less apparent. So, have a good day and just be you.

Good morning! Today's life lesson will add value to your life as the previous ones have. In this message, I will emphasize making the right choices. We need to realize the effect of our choices on our lives; if we do not invest a fair amount of time in making the right choices, it'll directly affect us, leaving us shattered and hollow. Therefore, always be available to invest in the big decisions. Last year, I made a choice because I realized that no matter how long we have traveled in the wrong direction, we can always turn around. Do not be shy about taking that first step forward, changing your life in a positive way. Have a wonderful day, and just be you.

Good morning! Today, let us decide to be patient and gentle because understanding is an art, and not everyone on this planet is an artist. The key to happiness is focusing on the path to being happy by finding someone who can understand you, console you and cherish your mood. Sometimes, when life hits harder in your face, don't be cruel to yourself. Be kind and gentle, and in that moment of chaos, stay silent and calm. Be kind to yourself, your spirit, and your heart. Have a wonderful day, and just be you.

Good morning! Today's piece of advice is to choose one thing in your life that soothes your soul and liberates you from worldly worries. I found music as my relaxing mantra. It is the one thing that helps me reset my mood with the timing of a great song. It comforts my soul, and I find my comeback. Select the right kind of music that suits your mood. For the moment, you either forget everything or remember everything that matters. Transform your tough moments into beautiful memories. Embrace and cherish all the moments that matter to you. Over the years, I have concluded that my happiness is an inside job; if I decide to be happy, I should have the power to face the challenges coming in my way. Have a great day, and just be you.

Good morning! Life is full of challenges and trauma, but challenges never represent failure; in fact, challenges are the moments in our lives that tell us the amount of strength we have. We need to understand that the challenges and obstacles make us strong. They open different pathways to success and refine us for our better version. Many times, we cannot make sense of the current scenarios, but in those moments, we learn to stay focused and calm. You can only thrive with calmness and silence, as they are the key to success and a promise of a better future. Those who make noise are not praised because the strong ones are the most patient ones. Embrace the smiles and the tears in your journey to success. Have a great day, and just be you.

Good morning! A couple of days ago, I reminisced over my past and a special decision that I made about a year ago. Life does not always go according to your plan. Sometimes, heading in a new direction can be scary. Until you realize you are heading toward a new and exciting direction that will have its rewards and its challenges. I have seen many more opportunities that turned out favorable for me that I took for granted in the beginning. Therefore, never miss any opportunity; sometimes, the things that we take casually are meant to be the turning point of our lives. So, embrace every new chance with hope, belief, perseverance, and trust in your ability to succeed. The choice is always the first step to believing. Just be you.

Good morning! I still remember one of my happiest moments from the past year. It was a year ago when I finally realized I had the courage and strength to let go of things. I could not change to let go of people who didn't want to change or listen to new ideas. A year ago, when I had a turning point in my life, an older and strong advocate of mine whispered in my ear that if they were talking behind your back, you are ahead of them; that resonated with my exact vision. From that moment on, I changed my take on things, and I found myself in utter bliss. Thanks to that individual. Have a great day, and just be you.

Good morning! Today's message is to look for the possibility that can give you peace. Sometimes, the struggle is peace. Sometimes, being in chaos and coming out of it all very successfully without harming anyone is peace. Do not get trapped with the appearance, and don't believe anything until you fully engage in that thing. All the obstacles in life are the same, but the way we deal with them makes all the difference in our lives. My challenges and my happiness have taught me that kindness is not only a reflection of our soul but also the path that leads to happiness and gratitude because kind people are the happiest and most grateful. Find your inner peace, your kind spirit, and your reflection of happiness. I assure you that all these factors will shine through your energy. Have a great day, and just be you.

Good morning! Today's advice is to have an understanding mind and a great ear. To listen well, you must restrain yourself from disagreeing, giving advice, or talking about your own experience. Sometimes, all you need to have been is a peaceful mind and a great ability to hear and gauge. Not every time does everyone need your advice for a reprimand, but sometimes we need someone to hear us out. Have a great day, and just be you.

Good day! Most often, we struggle to find love around us and many of our mornings being filled with heaviness and stress. Therefore, today's lesson will focus on spreading love, having a kind heart, and understanding human nature. We often underestimate the power of kindness; we devalue how a small compliment of someone can create a positive impact on one's mood. Have you ever has anyone compliment you for your looks or your dress? I bet it was the most amazing day for you. I will tell you a small step: every morning when you wake up, take out 2 minutes and stand in front of the mirror to appreciate yourself, to praise where you are and how far you have come, no matter if the accomplishment was small, it still was a milestone that you covered. Life is too short to regret what has not been done; now look at the wider picture, smile, and shine like a star. Have a great day, and just be you.

Good morning!! The past year has taught me profound lessons that will tremendously contribute to my life ahead. I have learned that life can change with no warning, no matter how prepared you seem to be. This is when I started the practice of my morning messages; it is the practice that started to be honest with myself. Sometimes, it might hurt to see the future with hope in pursuit of happiness, but being positive and hoping to do the best is the only way to enjoy life. I have seen many people complaining about their period of struggle, whereas if we look at the wider picture, it is the journey that counts, not the destination. The journey to struggle is burdened with many lows and highs that teach us the profound lessons of life. So always enjoy your journey, and do not ever underestimate your struggles. Have a great day, and just be you.

Happy sunshine! Throughout my life, I have observed people complaining about the toughness of life. Remember, life was never meant to be easy, and there will be battles that will drain you like anything, but never lose your motivation; in fact, whenever there is any slip, you should elevate your motivation even more. It will boost your confidence even more, and the destination will be easy to conquer. Every day will bring new challenges your way, but sitting back and crying over what has happened is not going to get you anywhere. So, get up, work harder than before, and draft your inspiring story with your own hands. Have a good day and just be you.

Good morning! Today, I will not impart any lesson. Instead, I will admire people who choose to shine after all the storms they have been through. This is the most incredible act one can ever do; to rise after failing is an act of supremacy and self-belief. Not everyone has the courage to rise above their circumstances, so let us admire those who choose to rise and shine. Have a great day, and just be you.

Good morning!! We do not need to resolve our entire lives overnight, and there is no need to feel ashamed about our current situation. Instead, let us concentrate on the small actions we can take today to gradually move closer to our desired destination. Progress may be slow and incremental, but by taking one step at a time, we can reach our goals. Initiating that first step may be challenging, but it is far better than remaining stagnant. Keep in mind that not everyone may believe in you, and that is perfectly fine. What truly matters is that, at the end of the day, you have moved one step forward, and the most important belief is the one you hold in yourself. Look forward, step boldly, have a fantastic day, and always be true to yourself. Just be you.

Good morning!! The meaning of a happy life is to love ourselves. It does not mean to overlook your flaws. It means to reprimand yourself whenever you feel you have made a mistake. Love is a powerful emotion that outshines every other emotion. When we choose to love, we choose to discipline ourselves, be kind to our loved ones, and bring happiness to their lives. Therefore, prioritize peace over everything, have a great day, and just be you.

Good morning! If I talk of the past year, it was quite a journey for me. I went through a number of incidents that included challenges, heartbreak, and whatnot, but I pivoted to a new way of thinking. Rather than complaining to myself about the adverse events, I started to contemplate what it was trying to teach me. I focused on the lesson, and believe me, each time I underwent misery, I got a great lesson out of it. Sometimes, this transformation might be daunting, but you need to remain steadfast and composed through a great belief system. You need to trust the process for yourself, believe in you. Choose to be brave enough to assume the challenges and extract a meaningful lesson from them. Embrace this new outlook of life today and just be you.

Good morning!! As mentioned yesterday, life is always in a state of change, presenting us with new opportunities and challenges each day. Today, as I reflect on life, I draw a parallel to a photographer with their camera. Like a photographer focusing on something beautiful or significant for the message of their picture, we navigate life, capturing both good and bad moments. It never operates the way we want it to, do your part, so leave the rest chance and circumstance. Be happy and optimistic. Have a good day, and just be you.

Good morning! Start your morning by doing any small task that pleases you. It can be preparing your favorite style of egg. Start today with the thought of knowing that you are a change agent; you are one of a kind with unique gifts and talents, and embrace your skills, your talents, and your spirit. Share a smile, a simple greeting, go celebrate who you are and what you have become, do a random act of kindness, and watch how it impacts your energy. Give yourself a reason to smile, to laugh, and to shine. Have a good day, and just be you.

Good morning, my friends! I used to think I could fix anything in my life if I just tried a little harder or gave it more time. It took me a long time to figure out that some things are not meant to be fixed. They are meant to be a lesson. Last year, I realized that affairs in life are to make peace and accept the way they are. When what matters to us is unmanageable, just trust your higher power and move forward knowing that we did the best we could do. Sometimes, the smallest step in the right direction ends up being the biggest step of your life, so tiptoe, if you must, but take the first step bravely. Just be you.

Good morning! Today, we will dive into the essence of freedom, the sensation of daring to dream big and soar to great heights. Let us explore the tangible experience of success and reflect on the intricate concept of happiness. Set expectations beyond your wildest imagination. Refuse to let others dictate your capabilities or allow their limitations to constrict your vision. By shedding all self-doubt and wholeheartedly believing in yourself, you can attain what you once deemed impossible. Just be you.

Good morning today feel your freedom to dream and set expectations beyond your imagination. Do not let others tell you what you cannot do. Do not let the limitations of others limit your vision. If you can remove all your self-doubt and truly believe in yourself, trust in you, you can achieve all that is possible. Make happiness a priority and be gentle with yourself in the process. The most important lesson that I take from my life experiences is not what I have been through in my life that defines who I am it is how I got through it that has made me the person, I am. I cherish every moment, I embrace every lesson, and I take a deep breath and enjoy every day, surrounded by happiness and joy. Hope is my fuel. My heart is my key, and my spirit is my vessel take today to remind yourself who you are, take care and just be you.

Good morning!! Today, I will share the most profound lesson of my life with you. A weaver once told me the story of Weavers and why they weave the stories behind the blanket jacket or bracelet. They said that life is not a picture of perfection. Rather, it is the weaving of imperfect moments. Life is a blend of good and bad days, and everything is designed to be artistically reflective so that when we ponder over it, we will only see its imperfect beauty. Happiness cannot be valued if you do not undergo the tough and challenging days of your life. Good days and amazing moments unfold an imperfectly perfect story like a finished beautiful weaving; believe that your life is a gift to the world; share it, embrace it, and live it without any fear or restraint. Have a good day, and just be you.

Good morning! Today is the most memorable day for me; it is the day when my son was born. Today, I was rewarded with the first gift of fatherhood and the greatest happiness of my life. That day, I discovered that life is a miracle and every breath we take is a gift from a higher power. Since that day, I decided that every day I would get up and be thankful for providing me with yet another day to conquer. Always believe that your inner spirit knows all your silent battles; your spirit is there to support and provide you comfort. Never think that you are alone because the truth is sometimes you just must do what's best for your spirit, your heart, and your soul. The strength of that choice guides you to the light of happiness and joy, and your willingness to hope imparts you with a superpower to weather the storm. With this, have a good day, and just be you.

Good morning! As I was traveling yesterday, I was reflecting on my life, and I said to myself, I am exactly where I'm supposed to be. Sometimes, struggles are what we need in our lives to shape us in the best way possible. If we go through our life without any obstacles, challenges, or random opportunities, we would not have the experience or lessons on how to deal with and overcome our challenges or push through opportunities or choices. We would not be as strong as we are today, so give every opportunity a push, push through every challenge so you do not leave any room for regret. Go, shine, celebrate, and be the real you without any fear of judgment. Have a good day, and just be you.

Good morning! I guess the real fact of the matter or my path this morning, is we do not know what tomorrow is going to bring us. The only thing that we know for sure is our present, so do not stay angry for too long, and accept the nonsense of the misinformed or the judgmental. Love your friends and your family with all your heart. Have fun and live your life the way you want to live it; most of all, do not worry about the people who don't like you. Enjoy the ones you do remember; the most important person is the person you see in the mirror. So, cherish your presence and who you want that person to be. Have a good day, and just be you.

Good morning! Yesterday, I took a personal day to reflect on the true essence of life. Today, I am embracing the present moment, acknowledging that happiness is not a distant destination but a daily choice. We have the opportunity each day to choose happiness. It is inspiring to observe those with minimal resources who still manage to wear a smile. In navigating our journey, remember these two guiding principles: be mindful of your thoughts as they shape your path in life, and exercise caution with your words, as once spoken, they cannot be taken back. You do not need to seek approval from everyone; instead, cultivate a kind personality and choose your words wisely. If a certain company does not resonate with you, gracefully part ways without the need for confrontation. Just be you.

Hello and good morning!! Yesterday seemed like an exceptionally long day. After driving all day long, I got home and thought about the importance of peace and happiness, and I realized that it comes from within. When you decide to love and respect yourself, you can live the most amazing life. One profound thing that I learned about happiness is that it should be independent of others. Yes, you read it right; your happiness should not be seeking anyone's support. You need to live life on your own without depending on someone. Live life as you want, but keep in mind, never go wrong with anyone, and be a peacemaker because the more you mess up, the more unhappy and unsatisfied you will become. With this piece of advice, have a wonderful day, and just be you.

Good morning! Today, let us celebrate for no reason at all. This celebration should be free from all the parameters that society has set for us; it should be totally for us and from us. Sometimes, the celebration does not have to be grand, it just needs to feel from within. It can be sitting alone in a quiet place with a cup of coffee and enjoying your solitude. Everyone has their own definition of happiness and celebration, and this is the beauty of uniqueness. Everyone has their own choice to live life, and this is where the beauty of individuality lies. I learned a lesson about choice; it came to me after a lesson of disappointment or disenchantment. I am not sure which for me, but it became a reassurance of my value. We must understand we cannot keep fighting for someone to be in our lives; if they are ok with losing us, we should also be okay with losing them. We need to learn our self-worth at all costs. I had to breathe and use a lesson of patience. Patience is when you are supposed to be mad, but you choose to understand and respect the choices of others, so embrace your values and accept who you are. Be the best version of you and, have a good day, and just be you.

Good morning! It is time to regain your strength. Happiness, grief, overthinking are the sentiments that we live through, and the worry of future and present is real, but let me tell you something amazing. Past and future do not even exist, yes you read it right. The past is what has passed and future is what has to come, what matters the most is the present. Present moments are what truly bring happiness to your life. If your present is good enough, then certainly your past will be left with some nice memories to hold back to. All you need to do is to be positive. When I was trying to comprehend this phenomenon, it took me ample time to process the phenomenon of past and present. And believe me that time was worth it. That day I made a choice to see things positively and have a positive outlook on life and here I am today amongst you all spreading hope and positivity. I passionately believe the day I changed my perception toward life, the universe turned in my favor and I noticed nothing but growth in my life. Have a good day and just be you.

Good morning! New mornings need to be filled with new reminders and today's reminder is to remain calm and composed. Today, I paused my pursuit of happiness and chose to remain steadfast in my purpose. Today, I will stop thinking and planning every step ahead and just walk in the direction my heart takes me to. I advise you all to enjoy your day, laugh to your fullest and stay calm and focused. Most importantly, just be you!

Good morning! Everything around makes sense if you have a positive mindset toward life. Today, I will impart the mantra of success. It is a tasty dish that takes in passion, patience, hope knowledge, keen awareness, hard work, and perseverance. I know the journey is not that easy, it feels daunting at times but the ones who do not lose themselves in the process are the true heroes. So, remain persistent with your goal, be clear and concise in your path and ace it. Have a good day and just be you.

Wake up my valuable readers! I made the choice a while back. The choice was to prioritize discipline over every other thing. To remain disciplined, the foremost act is to wake up early in the morning with a happy and cherished mood. In times of stress, I recall a message that is "this too shall pass" and this sentence comforts me immensely. Remember my dear readers, in this world, everything is temporary, what bothers you today, will not even matter tomorrow. After ten or twenty years, when you look back, you will laugh at your stupidity, how you would create a fuss over small things that don't hold any value to your present life. So, whatever feels overwhelming today, will fade away in the air and the life will be back on track. Claim your happiness today. With this have a good day and just be you.

Good morning!! Have you seen a tree with deep roots? What do you feel when you look at any gigantic old tree that has a wide and deep trunk? You must have noticed that every year, in the fall season, it loses all of its leaves, but it still does not collapse. It remains steadfast, exactly in its position and never complains. This should be the motive of us as humans, no matter what happens, we will not collapse, we will not hand over our happiness to that one moment that did not work in our favor. My dear readers, life is too short to complain and there is no use crying over spilt milk. The best way to utilize your past is to grab a lesson from your mistakes and implement the precautionary measures to avoid the same mistake again. Just be you.

Good morning! Let us start our day with a promise to be in a good place, to strive for better and not counting on our fate completely. I know many of us will find it offensive as some people blindly trust in destiny. Believe me we make our own destiny. When you observe the world, your brain gives you lots of messages and directions, the lazy ones do not bother to pay attention to its messages whereas the energetic beings contemplate and strive for betterment. The moment they think big, they have already taken a step further and the universe starts paving the way to success. True is the saying, "when there is a will, there is a way." The foremost component to success is to have the curiosity to change your present for good and just be you.

"Good morning! Today, I took a moment to inhale deeply and consciously opting for happiness. I recognized that to experience joy throughout the day, I must purposefully choose it. Regardless of the circumstances, we face each morning, whether positive, challenging, or neutral, we should not simply wait to discover the nature of the day ahead. Instead, we should actively decide the kind of day we want to have. Taking a pause, I breathed deeply, reset my mindset, and embraced joy and happiness. Wishing you a fantastic day, and just be you.

Good morning! Life's lessons revolve around discovering your true self and understanding what brings you fulfillment. Nine months ago, I felt shattered, losing hope, and sensing a broken spirit. It dawned on me that I had the power to change my situation, and the key lay in making a conscious choice. My heart became the engine driving this decision, emphasizing that healing, not merely fixing, was essential. I acknowledged a lingering hope for a brighter future for my children, my spirit, and myself. We all deserve peace, rooted in the tranquil and joyful state of our hearts, filled with love, happiness, hope, and joy. Life's beauty lies in its capacity for change, growth, and improvement. With this be happy and just be you.

Hello and good morning! Let us celebrate this new day as we continue the journey of discovering our true happiness. We are not lost in our lives; once we have created and recognized our happiness, no one can take it away from us. Remember, the mind is a powerful thing, and when filled with positive thoughts, you will find happiness. Have a fantastic day, just being you.

Wow, what a morning! I hope everyone is doing well, and we all find a reason to smile and embrace the new day. The simplest things in life, like a smile, a hug, or a random "I love you, Dad" or "I love you, Mom," a gentle peck on the cheek, are priceless treasures with immeasurable impact at the right moment. So, let us enjoy and embrace the simple things today. Someday, everything will make perfect sense, so for now, let us laugh and smile at the confusion, smile through the tears and frustration, and keep reminding ourselves that things happen for a reason. There is a purpose, a lesson; be patient, resolute, embrace the crossroads, breathe, and find your happiness. Have a good day, and just be you.

Good morning! Today I will tell you something funny about myself. My close family members and friends who know me well call me different. At first, I would laugh it off, but then I started contemplating the real reason, I looked back at my life, and I observed the key element that differs me from the rest. And that key element is my persistence. Many bad things happened to me, but I never gave in, in fact, it helped me regain my strength and I found a path in my life. A path of belief, a path of compassion, kindness, and generosity. When I started walking on this path, it made me different from others and people started liking me for my changed attitude. You can be the next person on the list, all it requires is to rethink your values and if you are already on the right path then congratulations. Have a good day and just be you.

Good morning! The right time reveals itself when our hearts shine with gratitude, our hopes soar, and our souls find peace. Patience and time guide us to our rightful place. Strength often accompanies those who have faced challenging pasts; what pulls us back to the past are memories and lessons. However, what propels us forward into today and the days ahead is our capacity to dream and hope. Take a step forward, breathe, have a good day, and just be you.

Good morning!! Let me tell you more about myself so that you can relate to me. I love the sound of rain on a spring morning. I have heard elders say that the rainwater cleanses everything, be it your soul, the dirt on earth, or the dust on trees. I liked the way they explained the phenomenon of the rain. I then noticed, is it important to pour rain to cleanse our souls? Can't we cleanse our souls without rainwater, then I realized that we are our rain water. We should not be depending on any other phenomenon to purify ourselves. It comes from within and those who don't want to improve, even the rainwater doesn't work, because it all lies within your soul. Have a good day and just be you.

Good morning! As I reflect on the growth of the past year, here are my lessons, thoughts, and notions that have anchored and focused me:

1-Train your brain to be stronger than your emotions; otherwise, you may find yourself lost in them.

2-Extend kindness not only to others but also to yourself; self-care is crucial.

3-Embrace life's challenges and difficulties, especially when undergoing personal transformation.

4-Maintain your daily perspective rooted in positivity; don't be disheartened by setbacks.

5-Recognize that true support is evident during life's storms, revealing who genuinely cares for you.

6-Amidst good intentions, remember that even a small step forward is more effective than grand plans without action. Stay happy and just be you.

Good morning! This morning, I encourage you not to doubt your strength. Even in moments of perceived weakness, there is a resilient force within you that refuses to give up. Always remember that beautiful things unfold when you distance yourself from negativity. Embrace your unwavering spirit of resilience, be strong, and move forward. It is time for happiness to find its way back to you. Have a good day, and today, just be you.

Good morning my lovely readers! Today, I will share with you all a secret that I have been observing over the years. I have learned many lessons from my elders, but this one hit me differently. It is about the death of my younger brother. My younger brother's death anniversary reminds me to reflect on the lesson I have learnt over the time. As time is more valuable than money because you can make more money, but you cannot get more time. A moment missed will not come back, this is why I value time more than anything. The pain of losing your beloved ones makes you stronger, in my case, it made me harder, and I noticed a change in my attitude. I heard somewhere that tears make you braver and I can now relate to this phenomenon very nicely. Heartbreaks make you stronger and I am thankful that my past has been a great lesson to me. I learned lessons that no school could teach. My past has been a guiding path for me and due to this, I am leading a content present and I anticipate the best for my future, but I do not stress for my future. I have left these affairs to my positive mindset, and as per my belief life is meant to be embraced, let us all embrace our present, learn from our past and lead a better future. With this, have a good day and just be you.

Good morning! Today, I have a simple message for you. Just learn that with every pain, there is a gain. If today, it seems difficult to you and you cannot see the things falling in place, believe that there will be a time, when the things will be in your favor. It is all about the perception, many people give into the process, and the successful ones remain persistent. They believe that things will change, the time will change and that their hard work will reach fruition. This belief of them differentiates them from the rest. I will suggest to all my readers to have a positive viewpoint towards your life, strive for betterment and the leave the rest on your mindset or your outlook on your life. Have a beautiful day and just be you.

Good morning! I thought to ponder over the relationships that play a crucial role in our lives. Sometimes, relationships appear as a challenge and it is hard to maintain a friendly bond with everyone around. When I reflect on the foundations of my relationships and friendships, the ones that truly matter to me. Those who played a significant role in making me who I am today. Reflecting, I realize that the best kind of relationship are not always your parents and siblings. To me, the best kind of relationship is the one that brings a change to your life and your attitude. Those who changed your perspective and contributed to making a better version of you. That kind of relationship is the best, it can be anyone, your friend, your siblings, your teacher, or a man once passed by. This is why I enforce the idea of acquiring knowledge, no matter who imparts it, as long as, it is important to you. Make the most of that information and spread the positivity around with your actions as actions are louder than words. With this cherish your day, and just be you.

Good morning my friends! Each day brings a new set of challenges, I don't know what's kept for you, I want to give you a message that might change your take on life. It may not solve your problem completely, I am sure, it will boost up your confidence and strengthen you to face the issue. In times of disparity, never lose your true self, always remain who you are and remain calm and composed. Always believe that this too shall pass. Do not take the decision that might affect you eventually, always think rationally. A strong heart with a good spirit will push through the temporary storms, they remain calm and composed believing that the times of hardship will end soon. Have a good day and just be you.

Good morning! Today, I will impart a valuable lesson to you all. It will be a little long so bear with me. Our life is not always about how we chose it to be, it works how our mindset and spirit chooses it for us. Always remember, you need to try in order to change your life but sometimes, you will see that your efforts didn't work out the way you deemed to. In those times, learn to leave it with your hope and belief system, and do your part and our part is to work hard and believe that it will lead to something good. I know it is not that easy, but this is how you make your life easier. Instead of wasting our time on the affairs that are beyond our control, we need to learn the art of "letting go." Believe me you will find it frustrating in the beginning but as the time passes, you will learn how peaceful it is to handover your affairs to higher power the power of your inner spirit. It will comfort your mind and soothe your soul. Grievances are real, make peace with the fact that grief and sorrow will create different versions of you for a brief period in your mind. But what truly matters in the end is who we dealt with in that situation. Be patient with yourself and breathe, take in the sunlight and blossom like a flower. Have a good day and just be you.

Hello my energetic readers! Some relationships in our lives hold prime importance in our lives, it can be your friends, your siblings, your cousins, or your colleagues. They are the ones who make our lives valuable and love us unconditionally. Sometimes, we fight with them over petty things because we trust them the most and we know that they will never leave us. But if things go beyond your control and you find out that this little argument will ruin your bond with them. Then the wisest step is to let go of that little thing and believe that this little sacrifice of yours will save your relationship with them. And this is the biggest blessing. Do not let your ego snatch your loved ones. It is OK to let go to cultivate deeper friendships. We all come to the calm or the end of a storm with the sign of a rainbow and sunshine. Good morning, have a good day and just be you.

Good morning! Celebrate this new day today with a powerful message. I had to remind myself that life can still be amazing and beautiful even when things do not go our way. And I want my readers to understand the very concept, an amazing life is not about how fairly it treats you, instead, it is about how fairly we treat life. Isn't it amazing? When life hits harder, we do not surrender to this easily, instead we make peace with the situation and live contently without any chaos. It shows our strength and commitment to ourselves. Sometimes, these hardships come to assess our patience and resilience, and the successful are the ones who don't surrender this easily. Their unshakable belief and calmness take the lead. Even after losing some battles, they win the major battles of life, and they might not be listed as the winner but they win the trust which is the most precious gem of all. Have a good day and just be you.

Good morning! Pericles, the Greek statesman said that time is a wise counselor. Benjamin Franklin said lost time is never found again and John F. Kennedy reflected on time by saying we must use time as a tool, not as a crutch. Rightly so, when I link back the events in my life, all these sayings by these wise men make sense and I feel blessed to comprehend their meanings. Reflecting on my life, my journey in the year has been a great lesson. It taught me to take care of the moments, my spirit. 25 years ago today, I received an early morning call from my sister telling me my brother had just died in a car accident. For the past 25 years, I have lived with the regret of not spending quality time with my brother. I never had the chance to tell him how proud I was of him or that I loved him. Many of my friends know me for my random road trips, one day, I left my office in Toronto and randomly ended up at my mom's home that was 6 hours away. I stopped at my mom's and my brother was not home, so I went driving around looking for my brother, I heard someone call out my name, I turned around and to my surprise it was my brother. We had a quick chat and decided to have a brother's day. In the morning, I decided to head back home. The next weekend I got that call. Be happy and do not cry over the things that are beyond your control. Time is a precious treasure that never comes back and for my workaholic friends, time is your friend not your enemy. Choose wisely, have a great day "miss you bro" and just be you.

Good morning! How would you feel if life brought us back the things that went wrong and we could get a chance to fix them up. We will be in bliss, we will not repeat the same mistakes but ironically, the world does not operate this way. What is passed, will never come back, therefore I say it to you all, make the most of your present and do not miss any single opportunity, as you do not know what it may have to offer. Have a good day and just be you.

We have come to the end of this book. The final message of this book is we may not have the life we want, but we can ensure to make the most of the life we have. Sometimes, all we must do is to forget what we feel and remember what we deserve. It is my reminder of why I love butterflies, the image of this book cover, butterflies are nature's gift. They remind us of the phenomenon that it is never too late to become the person we want. For me, I want to be the reason for someone's belief in good people, I want to be the ray of sunshine for someone today so that they can shine tomorrow and when they remember something about me, it is only the goodness of my character and nothing else. I hope you enjoyed the book and the next one is coming soon, and it is all about "Finding You".

Have a good day and finally just be you.

About The Author

Wayne Kaboni considers himself a social impact champion and entrepreneur. He is a thought leader and the principal of a few companies specializing as social economy companies and technologies company based out of Toronto.

Being an Indigenous social impact entrepreneur and now an author, he is guided by the principles of the Seven Generations teachings. Our land and history empower organizations to achieve success and acceleration by securing the idea that any goal is achievable with the right mindset. In addition to his busy business schedule Wayne has also served his community through volunteer work as a coach and board member. For the past 20 years his life was about being a good single dad raising his two sons and working for service organizations and providing oversight on the development and management of community trusts.

During Covid he developed 4iP a social media platform for Indigenous people globally that he financed and programmed along with a software partners. Indigenous Roots Radio is an online music streaming service for Indigenous musicians and song writers, we're songwriters and musicians benefit from the revenue generated from sales of their music and a percentage of the profits goes to the establishment of a Indigenous music trust to help support and develop new musicians further develop their skills and produce music. 4IP was established to give Indigenous people safe place to discuss and collaborate the issues, topics, projects, and community priorities. During the 90's tech boom Wayne was the CEO of Two Rivers Computers and Two Rivers Technologies based out of Ontario. His company was the first Aboriginal technology company to be awarded a National Master Standing Offer as an ISO 9002 computer assembler by the Canadian Federal Government.

He has recently completed his MBA at Thompson Rivers University/Nicola Valley Institute of Technology in British Columbia. The achievements of Wayne's career journey to date are vast, long lasting, and legacy enriching. It is these accomplishments and his strategic vision that have led to him being sought after for senior leadership roles in organizations. He has also been an instructor, coach and mentor for a number of youth hockey programs, and extensively active in the hockey and lacrosse associations in Ontario and British Columbia.

Manufactured by Amazon.ca
Acheson, AB